6-6-12   57854   Gift

Iwo Blasted Again

Ray Elliott

Tales Press
Urbana, Illinois

Address inquiries to Tales Press, 2609 North High Cross Road, Urbana, IL 61802.
Visit our Web site at *www.talespress.com*.

First Edition, 2006 by Tales Press, Urbana, Illinois

Library of Congress Cataloging-in-Publication Data
Elliott, Ray, 1940-
Iwo blasted again / by Ray Elliott. -- 1st ed.
p. cm.
Summary: "Story of an elderly Iwo Jima veteran dealing with memories of combat
and personal loss as he experiences a psychological phenomenon known as sundown
syndrome in the last hours of his life"--Provided by publisher.
ISBN 0-9641423-8-4 (alk. paper)
1. World War, 1939-1945--Veterans--Fiction. 2. Retired military personnel--Fiction.
3. Older people--Fiction. 4. Death--Fiction. I. Title.

PS3605.L4496I96 2006
813'.6--dc22
2006022206

Printed in the United States of America
Book design by Vanessa Faurie; Cover design by Carlton Bruett

For Bill Madden, E/2/27, Fifth Marine Division, Iwo Jima, who provided much of the background information, and the thousands of Marines with him who fought and died there; for my mother, who held the torch and lit the way in the aftermath; and for my young daughters, Jessica Page and Caitlin Storm, and young people everywhere that they may know the price of war and the freedom they enjoy.

Author's Notes & Acknowledgments

First and foremost, I want to acknowledge my deep appreciation and heartfelt thanks to William B. "Bill" Madden, a Marine veteran who served with Easy Company, Second Battalion, Twenty-seventh Regiment, Fifth Marine Division in the battle for Iwo Jima. His help on this book and his encouragement to me have been above and beyond the call of duty.

Bill landed with the first wave of Marines that morning in February 1945 and provided a great deal of the background information during the writing of this novella, openly sharing his experiences with me personally, on the telephone and by e-mail, without hesitation. He also gave permission to print his poem, from which I've taken the name for this book and fashioned the structure of this work.

I'd read a lot about the Iwo Jima campaign over the years and had talked to a number of combat veterans of the battle. The first was Oral "Ben" Correll, a man from my hometown who had been wounded on Iwo Jima, serving with Able Company, First Battalion, Twenty-eighth Regiment, Fifth Marine Division. I'd known Ben since I can remember, and from the time I was in high school, he'd patiently answer my many questions about his experiences.

Two of the Marines in his company had been awarded the Medal of Honor for their valiant deeds on Iwo Jima. One of them cleared the way across the narrow part of the island with a .50 caliber machine gun he called his "stinger" that he'd taken from the wing of a crashed Navy plane and modified it so he could hold it in his hands and fire it on the run. He died at the foot of Mount Suribachi near where Ben was wounded early in the battle. The other man lost his hands defending his outpost on the night he was awarded the Medal of Honor for stopping a night infiltration of a small group of Japanese soldiers. Sadly and tragically, years later, he ended up killing his wife, their neighbor and then himself in his Texas driveway.

After I came home from my time in the Marine Corps and up until just a few days before Ben died at sixty years of age, we talked about Iwo Jima and the Marine Corps many times. One of the last things he said to me as he lay on his death bed was, "Won't be much more time to talk about the Marine Corps."

He was right. They buried him a few days later, but I remain greatly indebted to Ben for sharing his stories with me.

Some years later, I wrote a story for the University of Illinois' alumni magazine about a deceased Navy physician's collection of letters from wounded Iwo Jima veterans that ended up being donated to the school by the doctor's heirs.

Dr. Luther Lowance, a graduate of Illinois, had instructed his nurses to take paper and pencil to the wounded who were able and have them write about their battle experiences, partly to give them something to do by occupying their time and clearing their heads, but also, I suspect, to record their thoughts and experiences for posterity.

One of the most poignant letters was written by a Marine, Sgt. William D. Norman, who was a veteran of prior campaigns in the Pacific and had landed on Iwo Jima with the Twenty-fourth Marines in the first wave of the reserve Third Marine Division. He spent several days in combat before being wounded and evacuated. His letter painted a picture of immediacy and eloquence that was vividly etched forever in my mind's eye.

"The sight that met my eyes as I set foot on the beach is one that I shall never forget," Norman wrote mere days after he was wounded. "Dead Marines were so thick that we had to sidestep them in order to move forward. I have withstood heavy enemy bombardment that lasted all night on Saipan, but never have I seen men who had died so violently. Men were blown to pieces, one leg here, an arm there, and strings of guts that were several feet long. These men had scarcely set foot on the beach. But to us, this was a reminder that we would have to fight, and pay in human lives and blood, for each foot of this barren island."

Later, Norman was one of the first Iwo Jima veterans to return to the island when the American veterans of the campaign participated in the Fortieth Anniversary Reunion of Honor and met with Japanese Iwo Jima survivors. This horrific battle had cost the lives of 6,821 Americans and nearly all of the twenty-two thousand Japanese who were defending the island.

At this point, I was actively seeking out Iwo veterans with the idea of writing this novella, and I was fortunate enough to have been invited to New Orleans to attend the fifty-ninth Iwo Jima Veterans Reunion. Unfortunately, Norman had died by that time, but it was there that I met Bill Madden, as well as his buddies, Hank Herandez and Al Pagoaga, from his old company. They were very generous with their time and their stories. And they introduced me to Keith Neilson and several others, including Jay Rebstock, whom I had the privilege to talk to only briefly on a few occasions afterward until he died two months after the reunion. I even met Al Hughes, a man who had served with my old friend Ben Correll in Able Company, First Battalion, Twenty-eighth Marines, and remembered him by the nickname he picked up in the Marine Corps — Smokey, after a popular cartoon character of the time, Fireman Smokey Stoves. I'd never asked Ben about his nicknames.

About the time I finished a draft of this book, I learned about a trip to Iwo Jima for the Sixtieth Anniversary Reunion of Honor. Putting my feet on the ground of Iwo Jima with Iwo Jima veterans was an opportunity I could not pass up. Walking among ninety-some elderly men who had stormed the beaches of Iwo Jima in 1945 as young Marines and hearing them talk about it as they stood on that very sand and rock was an incredible experience.

There was John Britton, who had almost the exact same name as my main character but whom I'd never heard of until I met him on Guam and walked with him on Green Beach where he'd landed with the Twenty-eighth Marines — he was graduated from the high school in Urbana, Illinois, where I taught for years and still reside; there was Albert Abbatiello, who had spent thirty-six days on the island and had been back the year before when he'd searched the caves where two of his closest buddies had been lost; there was John and Clinton Butler, both later-day Marines who had come to find the place where their father, Lt. Col. John Butler, had fallen while leading the First Battalion, Twenty-seventh Marines; there was retired Col. John Ripley, a Navy Cross recipient from the Vietnam War and Marine Corps historian who led the Butlers to the spot their father was killed; there was John Sardone, (Sgt.) Dewey Norman's company commander who had also fought at Roi Namur, Saipan and Tinian; there was retired Col. Gerald Russell, who had fought on Guadalcanal and became a battalion commander on Iwo Jima at the age of twenty-seven; there was Jack Lucas, who at fourteen years old had lied about his age when he joined the Marine Corps and had stowed away on the Iwo Jima-bound *USS Deuel* in Hawaii at sixteen. (He had gone ashore with the First Battalion, Twenty-sixth Marines and had received the Medal of Honor for jumping on two grenades and saving the lives of other Marines a few days after he turned seventeen.); there was Marvin Perrett of the Coast Guard who had landed troops on Utah Beach in Europe before being sent to the Pacific and landing troops on the beaches at Iwo Jima; there was Joseph Rogers, a San Francisco lawyer who had come back to the island he'd fought on after he had been seriously ill the year before and his medical doctor son had stayed by his bedside; there was Navy corpsman Danny Thomas, a Texas pharmacist who'd treated more than his share of wounded Marines a long time ago; and there was Arnold Shapiro, a television producer who had made two documentaries about Iwo Jima and had raised the money and written the inscription for the memorial overlooking the landing beaches.

All of these individuals and more have contributed in one way or another to my understanding of the Iwo Jima campaign. Without them, I could never have written the story I wanted to tell about what happened to them and how they lived with it. To the veterans, especially, I am eternally grateful for the honor of allowing me to ask the questions and to walk among them.

Back home in Illinois, Iwo vets James Kelly, Edgar Barstow, Roy Charles, Frank "Sammy" Weldon and Lawrence "Slats" Trower of the Richard L. Pittman Marine Corps League #1231 (named for a Marine who was killed at the foot of Mount Suribachi on February 21, 1945), all spoke with me about their experiences and memories of Iwo Jima. And John Hembrough, a Marine who lost a leg in Vietnam, and James Wright, a Marine who lost both arms in Iraq, shared their experiences about dealing with the loss of their limbs. They are a special group of Marines to whom I'm quite thankful.

In addition to the tremendous role Iwo Jima plays in this book, there are also the significant aspects of elderly care-giving and the psychological phenomenon known as sundown syndrome that was beneficial for me to learn about. It was my unsuspecting mother who taught me firsthand about that. She'd been in and out of hospitals for the better part of the past twenty years, and I'd been with her through several emergency room and ICU visits since she lived with me and my family for the last eight years of her life.

It was during one of her last hospital stay that I first heard the term "sundowner" as it applied to elderly patients, though most often associated with Alzheimer's disease. But the phenomenon apparently can affect other elderly patients who are ill, disoriented as to place and time, on medication, sleep fatigued or experiencing any number of other traumatic conditions.

As night progresses, people who exhibit sundowner characteristics lose track of time and place and become belligerent and often lose contact with reality. They're in the present one second and back several years in the past the next. And they do and say many things out of character that they would never do and say under normal circumstances.

My mother taught me many valuable lessons in the course of her life, and I know this was not one of her deliberate teachings. But she did instill in me a strong sense of duty and responsibility to family, and that is why I was at her side and experienced this phenomenon with her throughout some of her last nights. In a strange way, it formed another close bond between us, and I am especially grateful for the private time we had together.

As this book was completed, Bill Madden, Professor Emeritus George Hendrick of the University of Illinois English Department and my wife Vanessa Faurie have been invaluable with their editorial feedback for the final draft.

Many others read an early draft and wrote testimonials, including Miles Harvey, Kaylie Jones, Taylor Pensoneau, John Bowers, Walt Harrington, Jack Stokes, Col. Gerald Russell, Jon Shirota, Thomas Hollowell, Don Sackrider, Helen Howe, Jack Lucas, Joseph E.C. Rogers and Writer's House agent Michele Rubin.

My thanks to everyone, and my apologies to those whose names I may have inadvertently left out.

RAY ELLIOTT

IWO JIMA

Kat-ZOON! Kat-ZOON!
"Incoming!" I cry,
as fragments of mortars
explode into clusters of troops who explode into fragments
of flesh and sand and steel
which zing past my ears as
I dive like a fox for a hole.
Kat-ZOON again, and
a tardy stray locates my lair
and buries me there
with pieces of rifle
and shattered grenade;
my buddy Al helps rob the grave
of all but my ears
left buried there,
forever to listen for incoming calls.
My best friend Jim is shredded now;
I sit on my helmet and grieve as he dies.
Jim, my friend for life;
Well, there is still Al;
Yes, Al is still here.
We are still three, aren't we?
But no, not really three,
Al and me,
We're a ghost and two.
Jim is gone, mortar-blasted,
Iwo blasted, evil-blasted;
Just two survive, Al and me.
Then Al is gone.
The sniper chose Al, right next to me.
How could this be? We were three;
Now there's me,
Just me.
Why me?
Why?

— *Bill Madden, E/2/27, 5th Marine Division, Iwo Jima*

For just a fleeting second, the line on the heart monitor went flat. Then Jack Britton gasped for air, took a harsh, rasping breath and kept on sucking in the hot, dry air with a labored, hurried, irregular rhythm to take in enough oxygen to help his old heart pump another supply of fresh red blood out into his bone-tired, aching body again and make his leathery lungs crackle just a bit from the fluid that was staying in him. He felt tired, more tired than he had for years. And he had felt that way since he first awoke a little before midnight and knew something was wrong. He had had difficulty breathing and drifted in and out of sleep the rest of the night. His eyes opened now, narrow slits against the light of the early morning March sun that filtered into his little house through an east-side window, and locked in on an old photo at the foot of his bed. He couldn't quite make out what was there through his blurry eyes. He could see only a hazy image of the three young Marines indelibly burned in his mind, all squinting out happily and confidently from a faded print in a long-ago photo of them in dungaree jackets and trousers, hands on each other's shoulders, brash smiles on their faces. That would be Bake and Roc and him, he knew. Good buddies. They didn't come any better. Anywhere. Ever. A couple of men moved slowly beside him and kept talking to him in low voices. What they were saying wasn't always registering, although the old man could hear exactly what they were saying.

"Here, Mr. Britton," the chunky one with the close-cropped hair and thick arms and shoulders said as he closed the Velcro cuff over the old man's arm and slowly pumped it tight, "now let me get your blood pressure ... 240/120, pulse 110 ..." and then put his stethoscope on the old man's back, "okay, let me listen to you breathe now; take a deep breath ... again ... a little crackling in the lungs. Let's get that oxygen on him and get him out of here before. ..."

"... he croaks," the old man mumbled under his breath. "Incoming ... watch out, Bake."

The tall, thin black man looked at him, licked his moustache and the end of a yellow lead pencil and wrote something down in a notebook. Together then, the two men gently lifted the pad they had slid under the six-foot-one body and the not quite two hundred pounds of dead weight to the waiting gurney in one swift, sweeping motion. Outside, they rolled the gurney and the old man through the ambulance door and began to secure them for the ride to the emergency room. Jack closed his eyes and felt the poncho relax around him and overwhelm him with anxiety. He couldn't figure out exactly what was going on and where the Negro fit in the picture. Wasn't any of them in the company for sure. They had their own outfits in Pioneer battalions and motor transport companies as far as he knew. Even had a separate set of serial numbers. Something's not right here, he thought. What's going on?

He tried to look at his bloody right hand where the sniper's first round had hit, leaving the flesh hanging and fingers pointed every which way. But the shot of morphine was setting in and blurring his vision and sending him floating above the poncho on which he was lying. Somewhere close by he heard a voice that sounded vaguely familiar say, "We'll be right with you. Try to relax."

"Take care, Britt," another voice said. That sounded like Roc.

"Take care, my ass," another voice said in a thick Cajun accent, sprinkled with sharp grunts for emphasis. "We need him here on the line. Too many fuckin' men gettin' a little scratch and gettin' sent back to the beach. Ain't goin' to be nobody left."

"Fuckin' trigger finger is 'bout gone, Dubois," the first voice said. That had to be the corpsman, Doc Childers, not Roc. But he'd been right there all the time. "Took another round in his shoulder and some shrapnel in his foot. He's gone. No way in hell can he stay up here."

"No way in hell," the old man said and felt his nose tickle and reached to scratch it.

"That oxygen help?" the thick-chested man asked.

Jack nodded slightly and wondered what Dubois was doing. He was the squad leader. Didn't seem like he'd have time to be giving anybody oxygen. He had the squad, what was left of it, to keep moving up past 362A. Goddamn little Jap bastards popping up behind you, in front of you, everywhere and picking you off like flies or raining mortars in on top of you ... Bake was gone ... so were Greene and Kelly ... and Chernowski and Mathews ... O'Keefe and Robinson, too ... Jackson and Martinez never made it off the beach ... Jones and McCartney not much farther ... Larson — aw, yeah, Larson never made it off the beach, either. A burst from a Japanese Nambu machine gun opened him up like a zipper right there at the water's edge. Jack had dropped down beside him, braced for the rounds that never came and wondered what he could do. No time to help much; nothing that could be done about it, anyway, and he had to move on with people still on their feet. The second wave was landing and the third was right behind it. That's when the shit really hit the fan and the bottom dropped out all along the beach as the Japanese stepped up their resistance. Already then there were dead Marines everywhere, men blown apart, arms and legs scattered here and there, strings of guts stretching out for several feet, corpsmen treating men and getting hit by mortars and seventy-seven millimeter shells and dying with the already wounded before they had a chance to treat anybody.

And the situation only worsened. Japanese spotters began calling the mortars in on equipment and Marines with deadly accuracy while they were all bunched up on the beach. Navy battleships and Marine planes pounded the Japanese strong points in return. Gear was scattered willy nilly everywhere, M-1 rifles, Browning Automatic Rifles (BARs), machine guns, packs loaded up with shelter halves, blankets, shovels and three days of C Rations and canteens and ammunition and hand grenades — and gas masks which doubled as a life preserver. But they were strapped to one leg and buoyed it, making it more difficult to run through the water to the beach. Marines who were dropped out in the water in the amtracs started pulling their Ka-Bars and cutting the straps to the gas masks as they ran. That picture of so many steel-gray masks, like ghoulish heads, bobbing and floating en masse out to sea was stamped in Jack's mind forever, like the mark from a hot branding iron. And like everybody else, he'd cut his mask away and let it go before he reached the beach.

"We didn't need a life *preserver*," the old man said feebly. "We needed a *life* preserver."

Off to the left as he ran for the terrace, Jack heard another Nambu machine gun open up in enfilading fire from a bunker off to the right and above the terrace and saw the rounds tear the pack from a Marine's back as he dove for cover in the sand and stop another man in his tracks when the machine gun rounds hit him front and center. Jack dived and braced himself against the coming rounds. When nothing came, he was up and running again and again and again, joining up with the rest of his squad and taking the beach, up and over the terrace, and moving across the narrow part of the island with the regiment to where they'd turn north.

"Too many people didn't have one."

"What's that?" somebody said.

"Too many people didn't have one."

"Didn't have what?"

"Nothing," the old man said and stared hollowly upward. "Didn't have nothin'."

Inside the hospital emergency room, Jack Britton was hooked up to the heart monitor, his blood pressure taken again, and young emergency room doctors and nurses moved in and out around him with clipboards and stethoscopes, sticking a pill in his mouth — instructing him to "Hold it under your tongue"— poking an IV into his arm to send a clear liquid dripping into his veins, asking questions he couldn't hear clearly or just looking and using the situation as a learning opportunity for part of their medical training while they chattered in a language he couldn't understand and laughed about everything all at once like it was all funny as anything. Someone leaned over him and spoke slowly and loudly in English as if the old man were hard of hearing, asking him what his name was, did he know where he was and who the president was now. The old man laughed loudly once at the simplistic questions that were so obvious, and then ignored the man and the questions until he was told to roll over on his side and have something examined. The old man couldn't quite make out what it was that was to be examined and didn't much care. Then he felt something moving up between his legs and kicked out with both feet with all the force he could muster.

"Get that thing away from my asshole!" he said. "What the hell's going on here?"

"I was going to give you a rectal exam," the young man said. "I told you what I was going to do and why. You offered no objection, sir. We want to find out — "

"Is that right? Well, keep your finger out of my asshole. I'm gettin' out of here."

Jack could see people all around him through the narrow slits in his eyes he risked opening to see what was happening. Japs, slant-eyes. What's going on? he wondered again. What the hell are they going to do to me? The Japs towered over him, looking down at him with toothy grins. But there seemed to be nothing he could do about it; there was no way out. Roc and Bake and him had talked about their chances of getting off the island alive and about the possibility of getting captured and what would happen to them, if they did. No way did they want to get taken alive by the Japs. Nobody did. They'd heard stories about Japanese cruelty from the time the war started, from the Philippines to Wake and Midway and New Guinea to Guadalcanal and on to New Georgia and Vella Lavella and Choiseul and Bougainville and on to Tarawa and Roi-Namur and Guam and Saipan and Tinian to Peleliu— from all through the islands, they'd heard stories about men being beheaded or beaten to death, having their cocks cut off after they were dead and then shoved in their mouths or their tongues cut out while they were still alive and then bleeding to death or getting shot in the face at point-blank range, and they wanted no part of it.

Before the D-Day landing on Iwo Jima, it'd just been stories passed down the line from Marines who had fought in other campaigns. But when the company was pulled back for a couple of day's rest to recuperate after being hit hard just short of Hill 362A, Jack had learned that a man from the Twenty-eighth Marines had been pulled into a cave one day and thrown back out two days later, his fingernails pulled out, fingers broken, skull bashed in and more than twenty bayonet wounds in the stomach and upper chest with a final stab to the heart. The man's company commander, they'd heard from men in the company, had seen the body after it'd been tossed out of the cave and had talked with the Red Cross representative, a doctor and regimental liaison officer when they were there to file a report. The doctor was said to have reported that from the looks of the wounds, the man could have been alive and conscious for some of the torture.

Jack shuttered just thinking about it. He'd never seen anything like that. But they'd all had stories of Japanese cruelty pushed at them until they believed what they heard. By now he could believe anything. And some of the Marines were no angels, either. He'd never seen anything out of line

from the men around him, but he'd heard of Marines pulling
gold teeth from dead Japanese soldiers and keeping them in a
little pouch that was carried around the neck and collecting
ears from dead soldiers and carrying the ears on a string at-
tached to the cartridge belt as a coup of sorts for everybody to
see how brave these Marines had been in battle. Jack shuttered
again. And his head felt as if it were going to split open. The
excruciating pain soon spread across the lower part of his forehead just above the eyebrows, and he thought he'd taken another round or a piece of shrapnel. The morphine didn't seem
to be helping much. Touching his brow, he took his hand away
and saw blood rolling down his palm and onto his neck. What
the fuck, he thought. Jap bastards got me in the head, too. They
were gone now. He touched the compress that was taped to his
right shoulder and looked for Al Rocque. Guess I didn't pick
the right hole this time, Roc, old buddy. Not for me, anyway.
Got my ass shot full of holes is what I got.

But Roc was nowhere around. Maybe the sniper got him,
too, Jack thought. Some kid that looked a little like Roc stood
beside the poncho. He was looking down at the old man from
the bright lights above his bed. He'd seen the kid somewhere
before. He had the same full head of hair Roc had, only much
longer, and he had a long flowing moustache that reached out
to his sideburns. Fucking Roc's moustache was a little thin
one that gave him that Caesar Romero look, not this kid's Buffalo Bill look of "*Buffalo Bill's defunct who used to ride a watersmooth-
silver stallion and shoot onetwothreefourfive pigeons just like that Jesus
he was a handsome man and what I want to know is how do you like
your blueeyed boy now Mister Death*" from an e.e. cummings poem
he'd always liked and often had recited dramatically for his
literature students to grab their attention, sticking his index

finger out as if it were a pistol and using it to shoot the five pigeons as they crossed over the head of the students and dropped in front of Mister Death on the far side of the room. No, Roc must be off somewhere with his BAR zapping Japs as they popped out of caves or just jumped up out of the sand. Jack laughed at the thought. Wonder who's picking Roc's fox-holes and who's humping ammo for him now? Dubois must be having conniption fits from losing all his men. Hardly anybody left from the old company. Not even twenty of them left the last time he'd heard.

"How you feeling, Dad?" Jack Britton's son asked, standing beside his father's bed.

"With my fingers. How'd you think I feel?"

"I didn't know. I thought you were sick. Nothing wrong with you, I can tell. You're still in touch and on target. But they called and said you'd called 911 this morning. So I got here right away. You must've felt pretty bad to call. You seemed okay when I talked with you last night."

"Got hit pretty bad last night. Gettin' out of here."

"Got hit?"

"Yeah. Been in this hellhole sixteen days. Gettin' out."

"Oh, okay," Jim Britton said. "I see what you're talking about now. That's good. Glad you made it. How you feelin' otherwise?"

"Tired. I'm feelin' tired. Awfully tired. Got to get out of here."

"You will. Get some rest right now, though. Know who I am?"

"I 'magine. You think I'm nuts now, too? You're little boy blue, aren't you? Fast asleep in the haystack? *'Sheep's in the meadow, cows in the corn, Little Boy Blue's fast asleep in the haystack'* — Damn, my head hurts. Can you get me anything for this headache? It's killin' me."

"The nurse said the doctor ordered Tylenol for you awhile ago. Should be here soon."

"Yeah, that's what they keep tellin' me. Lyin' bastards. Can't believe a word they say. None of 'em. And you think I'm nuts now, huh? You're Tricky Jim. Who else would you be?"

"That's hard tellin'. Anybody you wanted me to be, I guess. What's going on? Have you had anything since you've been here? Pills? Shots? Tests? Anything?"

"They gave me one pill, and Doc gave me a shot for something awhile ago," the old man said and felt the tightness leave his shoulders and his mind wander away again, dreamlike but quite clear, back to a graduate seminar on the poetry of the Romantic Period: *"In Xanadu did Kubla Khan A stately pleasure dome decree: Where Alph, the sacred river, ran Through caverns measureless to man down to a sunless sea. So twice five miles of fertile ground..."*

— fertile ground, hell, Coleridge, Jack thought. Goddamn black sand ain't close to being fertile. It's a rock, a hellhole, full of nothing but killing and dying and not even twice five miles long. And more killing and dying. Killing or getting killed. Lucky I'm getting out of here:

Kat-ZOON! Kat-ZOON! "Incoming!" I cry, as fragments of mortars explode into clusters of troops who explode into fragments of flesh and sand and steel which zing past my ears as I dive like a fox for a hole. Kat-ZOON again, and a tardy stray locates my lair and buries me there with pieces of rifle and shattered grenade; my buddy Al helps rob the grave of all but my ears left buried there, forever to listen for incoming calls.

My best friend Jim is shredded now; I sit on my helmet and grieve as he dies. Jim, my friend for life; Well, there is still Al; Yes, Al is still here. We are still three, aren't we? But no, not really three, Al and me, We're a ghost and two.

Jim is gone, mortar-blasted, Iwo blasted, evil-blasted; Just two survive, Al and me. Then Al is gone. The sniper chose Al, right next to me. How could this be? We were three; Now there's me, Just me. Why me? Why?

"Why?" the old man said, muttering and his body relaxing as he dropped off to sleep, still thinking. Why indeed? Or why not indeed? Who the hell knows? Those kinds of questions would drive a man crazy, if he spent too much time thinking about them. Some people say they prayed and the lord saved them. But most everybody prayed. Why didn't all the prayers get answered? There weren't any answers. That's just was the way it was. The luck of the draw.

For a while the old man looked to be at peace, then he threshed around and woke sometime later, his head still throbbing, still wondering why and still wondering where Roc and everybody else was, why he wasn't with them, where he was and what he was doing where he was. He knew FDR was president; he knew that much for sure. Had been for a long time, for as long as he could remember. He laughed suddenly, remembering when they'd been in their foxholes with a full moon shining when Roc saw a man walking toward them. And challenged him. For the first three days on the island, the code word had been any American president; the next two days, it had been any American car; and the next three days, it was any American tree.

"I am President Roosevelt, I'm driving a Lincoln and I am looking for an elm tree," the man said and kept on walking as though he knew where he was and where he was going.

It seemed to the old man that he was in a wagon somewhere. He wasn't sure where he was going, though. The old wagon looked vaguely familiar, like the old corn-shucking wagons they used in the country when he was a kid and helped his dad shuck corn. He couldn't be sure if it was one of those wagons. But he'd been in the wagon before, somewhere. He was sure of that, though. A single rose stuck out of the ground a few feet beyond his reach. His head throbbed and ripples of pain shot through his temple every time his heart beat, but he felt somewhat at peace again and was still trying to decide where he was when a nurse entered the room with a small medicine cup in her hand. She shook the pain killer into his mouth from a small paper cup and held a somewhat larger plastic cup of water and a straw to his mouth for him to drink.

"This should help the headache, Mr. Britton," the nurse said. "Know where you are now?"

"Hell yes, I know where I am," he said, glaring at her. "You think I'm nuts, too? Everybody keeps asking me these stupid questions."

"Where are you?"

"Right here," he said.

"Where's that?"

"Same place you are."

The nurse smiled but didn't say anything more. She irritated Jack. But he was glad to see a woman. She even dressed and smelled and looked like a woman. Her blonde hair was drawn back and tied in a neat ponytail. A woman dressed like that meant he was probably somewhere off the island, he thought. He'd seen some women at the Fifth Division Hospital, but they were wearing rumpled dungarees and looked tired and worn out from the large number of wounded passing through on the way out or those that had to be sent over to the Fifth Division Cemetery.

"Are you hungry?" the nurse asked after he'd swallowed the pill. "I know you've been here awhile. We can order something, if you're hungry."

Jack shook his head. He hadn't been hungry for a long time. Nothing tasted good to him any more. The C Rations were okay if you were hungry, but he hadn't been hungry for the last couple of days. Lost his pack when Bake got hit and hadn't picked up another one. Didn't think about eating after seeing his buddy's head fly off and bounce and roll along the ground. Thought about other things. Thought about how his own mother would take it when she got the telegram that he'd been killed in action on Iwo Jima. Thought about how Betty would take it when she heard he'd be coming home in a box. Thought about Old Glory flying over Suribachi and about all the dead Marines he'd seen in the last couple of weeks who'd paid for that and so much more with their lives. Thought, too, about how he'd heard that a crippled B-29 returning from a bombing raid on Tokyo had made an emergency landing on the airfield on 4 March, long before The Rock was secured, saving the crew and the plane. Thought about how many more landings would be made before the war ended, saving more men and planes that were returning from bombing raids on Japan. Which was why they'd been told taking the island was so important. That first emergency landing was even before they'd carried him to the beach and loaded him onto the hospital ship, the USS *Samaritan*, on his way to Guam, before going on to Hawaii and the hospital in Oakland, California, and finally the Great Lakes Naval Hospital in Chicago and discharge. Jack smiled. It was good that they were already making those landings on Iwo and were saving lives and planes. That's what it was all about. It was good to know, too, that he was still alive and was headed off the island and back home. The telegram wouldn't say that he'd been killed now, only wounded. But Bake and so many more were long gone forever by then, Iwo blasted

and Iwo crippled or blown to bits in an Iwo second by an Iwo
mortar round that landed dead Iwofuckingcenter on him by
pure fucking chance. Took Bake's head right off. Jack'd seen it
rolling away in the black sand like a fallen rock, the eyes still
open with a look of horror in them. Bad luck for him, pure-
fucking-chance, shit-just-happens kind of luck. Life's an Iwo
bitch, then you fucking die like Bake and all the rest. Hundreds,
thousands of others gone forever. Just like that. What the fuck?
Chow didn't matter for nothing. No appetite.

"Don't want no Sea Rats," the old man said. "I'm hot, head
hurts like hell, mouth real dry."

"How 'bout some Jell-O, sweetie? That might help that dry
mouth."

"Might be all right."

"Strawberry be okay?"

"Yeah."

"Some Seven-Up?"

He nodded his head just enough that you could see it move
and closed his eyes. The morphine effect of numbing the pain
and making him feel as though he were floating just above his
rack seemed to be wearing off. Might get another shot at the
field hospital down on the beach, Jack thought. The pain in his
head pulsed with each heartbeat, and he felt sick to his stomach. His right hand picked up the beat. And so did the wound
in his shoulder and in his foot. Goddamn, Bake, why'd you have
to go off and get blown away? By a round from a Jap mortar?
Maybe by *"Fire and Ice"*? Like the poem I'd first heard old Jack
Frost — was that his name? I get confused these days by names
of poets. Was Shelley really named Bysshe? — read on the radio
once. Anyway, old Frost read the poem and I memorized it. Or
was it *"Fire or Ice"*? Either one would do the job. But a fucking

mortar? I think I know enough of death *"to hold with those who favor"* a bullet to the heart. The old man laughed. But if I *"had to perish twice, I think I know enough of"* war *"to say that for destruction"* mortars are *"also great and would suffice."*

"This'll have to suffice for now, Dad," Jim said, holding a spoonful of strawberry Jell-O out for his father to eat. "It's Jell-O. You said you wanted some. Here, sit up and take a bite."

Jim helped his father sit up, and the old man opened his mouth and took the Jell-O, rolling it around in his mouth and chewing slowly as if he hardly had the energy to move his jaws. Another small bite, a sip or two of Seven-Up and he sucked in a breath and shot out a stream of reddish liquid flecked with pieces of the strawberry Jell-O that hit the bed at his crotch and dribbled all the way back up to his neck as he lay back. More fucking blood, Jack thought. These holes just keep opening up. They plug one up and another one just pops open.

"Move out," he heard Dubois say to the men left in the platoon. "We ain't got all day."

Jack watched as the men moved out and then looked back toward the beach where he and the other wounded were headed. All the way back, he heard the su-woosh of the 3.5 rocket launcher, the old bazookas, the steady rat-a-tat bursts of the .30 caliber machine guns, exploding grenades, occasional fiery blasts from the flamethrowers that sounded like the blast from a hot air balloon that gave it a thrust upward, and the return fire from the Japanese Nambu and heavy machine gun fire and constant artillery fire from a piece hidden away in the caves that dotted The Rock, some rolling out on a track to fire the round, then rolling back inside to hide away and reload. He heard the rounds from the Navy's long guns out at sea that came whistling in any time and hit anyone who just happened to be there at the time. He knew he would never forget the un-mistakable Kat-ZOON of mortar shells that always came fly-ing in and once exploded into a squad of Marines grouped together and then the zing of fragments of body, sand and steel flying past his ears as he dived for cover. When he looked back at his squad again, he saw men fall and felt lucky not to be with them, sad that he wasn't there to be with them. That's where he really belonged, with Roc and Bake and all the others. He wanted to leave but didn't want to leave them, wanted them all still to be there for him, all to be there for each other.

With the morphine lifting him off the ground and above the fray, he could again see the ongoing battle for The Rock for a moment. He hadn't seen the flag go up that day, but he'd heard a low roar spread across the south end of the island when it did, heard somebody say, "There goes the flag," and looked up at the same time thousands of other Marines had and joined in the shouting until a loud roar could be heard above the din of battle. And the big ships out at sea had started blowing horns and sounding whistles when the men aboard ship had spotted the flag. Jack heard it all again and saw the flag waving there on Suribachi. What a beautiful sight! What a glorious sight!

"Won't ever see anything like it again," the old man said, smil-ing weakly. "Never in a million years. What a sight for sore eyes!"

"You sure are," Jim said, chuckling as he watched the nurse clean up the Jell-O barrage and acknowledged her work. "Thanks for your help."

The young woman smiled and nodded.

"Thanks, Doc," the old man said.

"This is your doctor, Mr. Britton," the nurse said and pointed to a small, dark-skinned man who had just walked up to the bedside. "Dr. Yasunaga. He's here to see you."

"Yasunaga?" the old man said and his body stiffened. His eyes could not quite focus on the doctor or what he was saying. But he was obviously Japanese. Jack knew that. What the hell happened? How'd he get here? Had he been captured? Where was the rest of the squad? Where was Roc? They had to be nearby. Roc had been right beside him. Off to the left and up the hill, Jack saw a Jap soldier start to run out of a cave just as the end of the flamethrower's force hit the entrance. The fiery blast pinned the soldier to one side of the opening and burned him to a crisp while Jack watched and heard the blood-curdling scream. He could see the shape of a man, all black and transfixed, standing where the force of the fire had caught him and impaled him. Jack shook and looked away. He'd never really questioned what he and everybody else were doing in the war. It seemed necessary to be fighting, even though he'd never completely gotten used to such random violence. Violence, down and dirty at every turn, at any time and at every place. Kill or be killed. But why'd it have to be this way? Why'd there have to be so much killing and dying? Why, why, why? Truth be known, the Jap soldiers probably felt the same way. The dying Japanese at the mouth of the cave burned brightly, his last dying scream fading away as the fire died out and he pitched forward. A helluva way to have to die.

"A helluva way to die," the old man whispered and opened his eyes and shook all over. Someone stood over him again. He couldn't tell who it was this time. His eyes just couldn't focus no matter how hard he tried. Didn't care.

"You look upset, Dad," the voice said. "Troubled. What's the matter? What do you want?"

The old man hadn't heard clearly and didn't feel like talking to anyone. He was troubled. No question about that. He'd seen death in so many forms he couldn't count them, still saw them in his head all the time. Dead buddies blown apart, dead Marines with their guts strung out on the dirty black sand, dead Japs bloated and busted with maggots crawling around on them and then one burned to hell and gone before his eyes. And there was much he couldn't see. Demolition squads set charges in caves and sealed them off, killing hundreds or even thousands of Japanese soldiers who refused to surrender. Everybody fucking dead and gone to hell. Iwo blasted. Dead, dead, dead, dead ... so many dead Marines that you have to step over them to move on. And you had to move on. Marines coming in behind, Japs out front. Japs behind. Japs all around. And now a Jap doctor. Jack saw faces of his buddies float in front of his face and look down.

Larson went down right beside him. Goddamnit to hell. Jack kneeled beside him as the platoon moved up on the beach for the terraces. All the rounds being fired off and mortars exploding and people hollering and screaming around him drifted away to the background. He heard Dubois bellow out to move on. "Move out. We've got to get off this fuckin' beach," the Cajun said. "We're goin' die right here, if we don't." But the kid was down. He'd been machine gunned and ripped open as he ran right into a burst from a Japanese Nambu. Blood oozed out and soaked through his dungarees and down into the black sand, making a reddish-black, sinister-looking goo that mixed in and became part of the bloody sands of Iwo Jima forever. What could he do? Larson's eyes were glazed over, but he knew he was dying and screamed out again, writhing in pain and fear. Jack realized the kid was dying, too, but knew there was nothing to do but shove off. He gave Larson his canteen and sulfanilamide tablets for the wound and the pain, looked at the kid, just seventeen, one last time and sprinted to catch up with Dubois, Roc, Bake and the others as he was ordered to do. It was tough to leave the kid alive. He'd squeezed Jack's hand but couldn't talk. Nor could Jack say anything. And he couldn't look back as he ran forward. He felt horrible, terribly guilty about leaving the kid there to die alone and couldn't bear to look at him again. What else could anybody have done, though? Nothing, he knew, not a goddamn fucking thing. But Larson was fucking dying, dying alone there on that godforsaken beach before the corpsman would ever get to him and before he'd ever know more than a few more painful minutes of life amid the battle for the beaches with hundreds of others dying all around him. Jack had braced himself when he saw Larson get hit and fall and braced himself again now, running and waiting for a round to hit him any time. How could he not get hit? Not get badly wounded or killed? How could anybody escape all the rounds and shrapnel flying through the air? Blood and guts everywhere. Arms and legs. Bodies ripped in half. Men dying, screaming out in pain.

"Aaaaaahhhhhhhhhhhh!" the old man screamed out and opened his eyes to see the Japanese doctor looking down at him. What was going on? Where was he? "Get away from me, you son-of-a-bitch, get away. I don't know a goddamn thing, so shoot me."

"Nobody's going to shoot you," the doctor said quietly. "We're going to help you get better. So you get some rest now, and I'll see you in the morning."

"Not if I see you first, you Jap bastard," Jack said. "You might as well shoot me now."

Somebody was wiping the blood from his shirt and holding a small pan that had more blood in it. A young, blonde-haired nurse wiping the old man's face and mouth with a cool rag was talking quietly in an accent he couldn't quite make out. It wasn't Japanese and neither was she. That was a good sign. Everybody seemed to have an accent of some kind, though. But he smiled at the sound of the woman's voice. He'd made it off The Rock and was going to have his wounds taken care of. He hadn't died there; he hadn't died yet.

"I'm still here," he said, whispering, sitting up in the bed now, holding his head in his hand with his eyes closed and reciting an old saying he'd thought about himself. "Fuckin' teeth in a glass, chest cracked open and shut back tight again, ears on the table, but I'm still here."

The young woman smiled again.

"Yes, you are," Jim said, standing at the side of the bed and laughing. "You're definitely still here. I figured you would be, didn't you? You're a survivor, Dad. That's what you've always told me, isn't it? That you're a survivor? Now just lie back and see if you can get some rest so you can keep on surviving, and we can keep you around awhile longer. Rest. That's what the doctor ordered. And you're tired, you said."

"Yes, tired. Tired as I can be, tired as I've been for a long time. Real tired when I woke up last night. Gettin' dark again, too. Daylight's bad enough, but nighttime is hell."

Darkness was coming when Roc and Bake jumped in a shell hole and started setting up for the night. They had an open area to the front, a good field of fire and a clear hook-up with the company perimeter. Just as they were settling in, Jack rolled into the hole and up against them.

"Welcome to my humble abode, Britt," Bake said. "What the hell you doin' here?"

"Ski got hit."

"Yeah. Too bad. Stay with us tonight."

"Right."

"Could I get you a martini? A cigar?"

"I don't like this fuckin' place," Jack said, looking around. "Don't like it at all."

"Is that right?" Roc said. "Just what is it that you don't like about it, Mr. Britton? Hell's bells, I thought this was the kind of place we've all been chompin' at the bit to get to all day. Looks like the Copafuckin'kabana to me after where I've been. No clean linens, looks like. C Rats to eat. Funny-tasting water to drink. But don't you just love the aroma of this tropical paradise when it ain't cold and raining? Aw, and the smell of gunpowder and high explosives day and night! You can't beat it anywhere. Beautiful black sand and lovely well-littered beaches to stroll on. Where else could you find to spend your nineteenth birthday so good, humpin' across those sandy beaches of Iwo-fuckin' Jima with fireworks goin' off all around you, welcomin' you to the party of your life. That's what it is, ain't it? Your birthday when we got here and the Iwo-fuckin'Jima Party to celebrate it? Goin' to take us three days to take this fuckin' little island, seventy-two hours, three days and nights and light casualties. Wasn't that what the fuckin' brass was tellin' us? Piece of cake for us bad-ass, fuckin' Jarheads, they wanted us to think. Somebody's always bullshittin' us somewhere, about something, fuckin' with our minds. How many days we been here now, Britt? Fifty, a hundred? And now you're tryin' to fuck with our minds."

"You're nuts, Roc," Jack said. "I don't mean this goddamn rock; I mean this goddamn hole. Let's move to that one up just ahead and a bit to the left. I like it better."

"Oh, you like it better. You like it better, do you? Let me tell you, buddy, one hole in this fuckin' place is just as bad as any other fuckin' hole on this rock. There ain't no high-rent district here, buster, and I ain't movin'. I'm as close to them fuckin' Jap caves over there as I want to be for now. We don't have to move, dig or do a damn thing except settle in and keep our eyes and ears open. I'd like to get a little shut-eye tonight without having some goddamn Jap crawl in the hole with me and try to cut my goddamn throat. I've had enough of that shit to last a lifetime."

"I'm with you, Roc," Bake said. "We're already here. Why the fuck move?"

"Because this hole just don't feel right," Jack said again. "Don't know what it is. Something about it don't feel right, and I'm getting the fuck out of here right now. Come on, so we can get a little shut-eye."

"It 'don't feel right!'" Roc said. "Did you hear what the man said, Bake? It 'don't feel right.' Let me tell you, Britt, ain't nothin' about this fuckin' little island that feels right."

Bake just laughed and peered out into the coming night. With three of them in the hole, they all agreed they'd be able to get a little more sleep and still have two of them on watch most of the night. But a hole was a hole, Roc said, over and over, each offering only the slightest cover. Jack just didn't feel good about this one. And in the end, Bake and Roc went along with Jack's feeling and moved up to the other hole. They didn't see any difference. They could still hear Jap soldiers all around them throughout the night, hollering out some insulting phrase or laughing maniacally and screaming, "You die tonight, Mlarine."

"Not if you die first, asshole," Bake had said once when he heard someone shout it out not far in front of their hole. "You die tonight for that fuckin' Tojo. How 'bout that?"

"Aaaaaaaaaaaaahhhhhhhhhhhaaaaaaaaaaaaa," a Japanese soldier was heard laughing. "You die tonight for that fluckin' Flanklin Rlooslvelt, Mlarine."

"So you like this hole better, huh, Britt?" Roc asked. "Listen to that shit. Ain't this place just special, Bake?"

"Yeah, sure is, Roc. Let's invite them bastards in for a tea party. How 'bout havin' some sake, too? Get everybody all fucked up and call off the war. Might be able to get some shuteye."

But nobody got much sleep. When it was relatively quiet, they'd think they heard somebody crawling out in front of their position and they'd wait and watch for the enemy who never came. And Japanese artillery lobbed shells in sporadically throughout the night. When they heard the whistle and swish-swish-swish of incoming rounds, they hugged the dirt and waited until the shrapnel quit flying and the sickening loud Kat-ZOON of the explosion died away. A couple of times it sounded as though the shells were coming in right on top of them but only brought showers of sand fanning out from an exploding round.

"Goddamn, that was close," Roc said. "Way too fuckin' close."

"Sure was," Bake said. "Any closer and Britt's fuckin' lucky hole kills us. You tryin' to kill us, Britt? They've got us zeroed in, looks like. Next fuckin' round is right on top of us."

"You have a choice of any hole on the fuckin' island, buddy," Jack said sullenly. "I'll refer you to my real estate agent from now on. He'll be glad to show you any number of new and improved developments. They're being made even as we speak."

A swish-swish-swish signaled another incoming round, and the three stretched out flat and hugged the sand. The round came in almost on top of them, digging another deep hole and sending a cloud of sand and rock flying through the air. After the sound of the loud ear-splitting exploding Kat-ZOOOOOON of the round died down, Roc hollered out, "You guys okay? I just about got buried by this fuckin' sand and dirt."

"Me, too," Bake said. "What about you, Britt? You still like this shit-hole?"

No answer.

"Britt!" both men shouted at the same time. "Britt! Where the fuck are you?"

"He must be buried over here, Roc. Bastards got Britt. Fuckin' slant-eyed bastards!"

"Let's get him out," Roc said at the same time, scrambling to the pile of sand where Jack had been when they heard the round coming in. "Goddamnsonuvabitchin'fuckin'Japs! They got Britt, they got Britt! Goddamn, goddamn, goddamn. ..."

Both men attacked the pile of sand side by side, digging with their hands, all the time cursing and crying. When they felt Jack, they started pulling together and dragged him out of the sand. He shook his head and coughed, blowing the dirt from his throat and nose.

"You all right, Britt?" Bake asked. "You all right?"

No answer.

"Talk to me, Britt," Roc said. "Talk to me, goddamnit."

No answer.

"He can't fuckin' hear," Bake said. "Explosion must've busted his fuckin' eardrums."

"I can't hear a goddamn thing," Jack said loudly, coughing again and spitting out black sand and dirt. "Got my fuckin' ears."

All he could hear was a ringing in his ears. He knew a little luck and a lot of Bake and Roc had saved him from certain death and huddled together with them for the rest of the night. Over the next two hours, his hearing gradually came back to the point that he could talk with them and hear what they said, but he knew that he would be forever listening for incoming mortar rounds. At first light, Bake looked back toward the beach and the first hole they'd jumped in the evening before. The spot had taken a direct hit and was twice the size it had been.

"Holy shit," he said. "Look at that hole. We'd be dead meat, if we'd have stayed there."

Roc's face looked drawn and a bit pale, but he smiled and then laughed way loud and the sparkle came in his eyes the way it did when he saw or heard something funny or witty.

"You can pick out my holes for the night from here on out, Britt, old buddy," Roc said after he quit laughing. "You just tell me where to go, and I'm gone; you tell me to shit, and I squat and say what color. Whatever you say to do, I fuckin' do. You saved our asses, buddy. You're clairvoyant. I want to stick with you. But damn, I'm tired now, and it's only morning. Wonder what that fuckin' Dubois and them fuckin' Japs got in store for us today?"

A slight smile tugged at the corner of his mouth again, and he shook his head.

"Thanks for pulling me out of what could have been my grave last night and saving my ass, too, boys," Jack said, "I would've died there." He felt a smile tugging at his mouth, also, as he remembered a poem he'd read in high school that had always been a favorite of his.

"'I have a Rendezvous with Death at some disputed barricade,'" the old man started whispering, "'when Spring comes back with rustling shade and apple-blossoms fill the air—I have a rendezvous with Death when Spring brings back blue days and fair....'"

He saw that kid standing there at battalion aide again. Or maybe this was the Fifth Division Hospital; Jack wasn't sure which one. He was lying there on a cot, half awake, semi-conscious and watched the people in white coats move around him and in and out of the door. The kid was smiling down at him and moving his mouth as though he were talking.

"... you're reciting that old Alan Seeger poem you used to quote all the time," Jim said and started the second verse but waited for the old man to pick it up: "'It may be he shall take my hand And lead me into his dark land And close my eyes and quench my breath — It may be I shall pass him still. I have a rendezvous with Death On some scarred slope of battered hill, When Spring comes round again this year And the first meadow-flowers appear.

"'God knows 'twere better to be deep Pillowed in silk and scented down, Where love throbs out in blissful sleep, Pulse nigh to pulse, and breath to breath, Where hushed awakenings are dear ... But I've a rendezvous with Death At midnight in some flaming town, When Spring trips north again this year, And I to my pledged word am true, I shall not fail that rendezvous.'"

"I won't either, by god," the old man said.

"I'm sure you won't," Jim said. "None of us will."

"But that wasn't the time for me, back then."

"No, it wasn't."

"It's coming, though."

"Not right away. Not this time, either. Didn't think I'd remember that poem, did you?"

The old man smiled weakly. "You've got a poetry nut for an old man, don't you? I always liked words and how they sound together. Ever since I was a kid. Still do. Reason I liked to teach. I wanted to pass along my love for poetry to young people the same way it was passed on to me. We had to memorize poetry when I was a kid. They don't do that any more. But I remember one time in school when we were studying the American Revolution. Mr. Abraham read Longfellow's '*Paul Revere's Ride*' when he talked about the beginning of the war and how it started. The poem was so beautiful and lyrical, the cadence of the words so right for the story of the Colonists fighting the British for independence. I loved the way it sounded and what it helped me see. It put me right there where I could see the history of our country more clearly: '*Listen, my children, and you shall hear Of the midnight ride of Paul Revere, On the eighteenth of April, in Seventy-five, Hardly a man is now alive Who remembers that famous day and year.*'

"See? You're starting right there on the horse with Paul Revere at the beginning of the poem and at the beginning of the American Revolution. And Longfellow went on to paint a terrific picture with his poem that's good for kids to see, grounds them in the early history of the country and prepares them for all that follows. Helps turn them on to poetry, too.

"'*He said to his friend, "If the British march By land or sea from the town tonight, Hang a lantern aloft in the belfry arch Of the North Church tower as a signal light, — One, if by land, and two, if by sea; And I on the opposite shore will be, Ready to ride and spread the alarm Through every Middlesex village and farm, For the country folk to be up and to arm...,'"* uh, oh, I can't remember how that goes anymore. It's gotten away from me. And I'm tired. Real tard. T-a-r-d. Don't get any rest here, don't get any sleep. Got to sleep."

He closed his eyes and felt his body relax.

"Hey, Dad, you're a Marine," Jim said. "Remember? Go on. You can remember."

The old man opened his eyes and smiled. Yes, he remembered the Marine thing very well. He used to laugh and tell the boy, "We're Marines," when the going got tough for them or life wasn't going too smoothly in the early years. "We can do anything, don't you know?" he'd say. "We're supermen. *'Faster than a speeding bullet! More powerful than a locomotive! Able to leap tall buildings in a single bound! Look, up in the air! It's a bird! It's a plane! It's Superman!'* No, wait, it's not Superman. It's the Marines!" They'd laugh and say it again together. It always helped them get through about anything.

When Jim was a sophomore in high school, he had had an operation to correct a severe overbite he had developed during the rapid growth of his early years. Besides correcting the overbite and heading off problems with arthritis in his jaws later in life that the orthodontist was primarily concerned with, the surgery gave the boy's face a handsome look that gave him the self-confidence he'd been lacking before the operation. That was after he had healed and had been through the six weeks with his jaws wired shut, existing on what he could suck through a straw or slurp from a spoon. During the eight-hour operation, the lower jaw had been broken and moved forward and bone chips taken from his hip and his upper jaw cut away and bone chips inserted to lower it a bit for alignment.

When Jack saw his son in the recovery room after the operation, Jim's face looked like it had been kicked and severely stomped on in a long, tough, knock-down, drag-out barroom fight. His eyes were swollen shut, his head and face had ballooned up to the size and shape of a football, his jaws were wired shut and he had tubes running down his throat and up his nose. Jack gripped the side of the bed rail and sucked in a sharp breath. He'd seen all kinds of wounded men on Iwo and in a number of hospitals through the following days and months. That had been bad. But he had showed little emotion at the time. That was just the way things turned out for everybody. It was different now. And it was his son who was the one who was hurt. As Jack stood beside Jim's bed, all choked up at the sight of his child battered and bruised almost beyond recognition and not knowing what to say but not wanting to sound stupid or hokey, he could only muster something about his son being brave and handling the operation very well.

"You're a brave kid, Jim," Jack said, remembering Arnold crawling back to the lines so battered they hardly recognized him. "I don't see how you do it. I'm real proud of you."

Jim pointed at his father's arm and tried to say something.

"The time?" Jack said. "It's about 4:30 in the afternoon. Been a long day."

Jim shook his head and pointed at his father's arm again and reached out to push back his shirtsleeve. Thinking the boy wanted to see the time for himself, Jack turned his wrist around for his son to see the time. He shook his head again. This time he pointed at the USMC tattoo in old English script on his father's forearm and then back at himself.

"You're a Marine?" Jack said, tears welling up in his eyes. "What a brave Marine you are, too, what a brave one. Bake and

Roc'd be proud of you, too. I, uh, don't know what else to say."

Jim had nodded slightly then, his eyes watering now as he stood beside his father's bed and remembered. He'd been told about Bake and Roc many times and how his father and mother had decided to name him James Albert after the buddies who had saved Jack's life and then had been killed on Iwo Jima while Jack somehow had survived and got to live his life.

Tears filled the old man's eyes as he tightly held onto his son's hand.

"It's hell to live when the others don't," the old man said and slowly let go, the tears still streaming down his cheeks. "Got to sleep before we have to move out again."

"What about the rest of 'The Midnight Ride of Paul Revere'? You just got started."

"I memorized the whole thing in school, all twelve stanzas. Mr. Abraham had me say it at a school assembly. Made me feel like a million dollars."

"I always liked to hear you say it. Can you recite the rest of it now?"

"No, probably not, Tricky Jim. I'm about done. Mind's going. Wanders. I can't remember a thing sometimes. And I'm tired. Tired as I can be. Tard. T-a-r-d. I need to sleep."

"Okay. Get some rest then. I'll be right here."

Getting some rest wasn't something the old man had been doing much of for a long time. For the first forty or so years after the war and his wife Betty's death, he worked to finish his teaching degree, raise Jim and be the best teacher he could. He hadn't talked much about the war through the years and said nothing about Betty to anyone except Jim. She'd been Jack's pick for a girlfriend since he'd first noticed her back in freshman year of high school. They used to talk in the library every day and got to know each other very well. But it was the summer of their junior year of high school before he finally got around to asking her to go to a movie one Saturday night. When he heard her say yes, he felt so good it was almost like he was walking on air. On the way to the movie, he told her about his plans after high school and what he wanted to do with his life. The war had just started, and he told her how he planned to join the Marine Corps like some others they knew, fight the Japs until the war was over, then come back and go to college to become an English teacher in some high school. He'd never forget what she'd said:

"That sounds wonderful, Jack. Have you ever thought of having anybody with you?"

"Yeah," he said and blushed, "somebody like you."

"Yeah," she said and blushed but reached her hand across the table to take his. "That's just what I was thinking, too. Not just somebody *like* me, though. Me. *Just me.*"

He blushed bright red and squeezed her hand tightly.

The memory of that night always brought a smile to his face whenever he thought about Betty. And he thought about her every day. Never a day went by that he didn't recall something she said or remember that special smile she wore on her face that could turn into a snarl in a heartbeat when something happened to call it up, like the time she thought he was flirting with another girl in front of her. Sometimes he imagined she was still right there with him just like he imagined Bake and Roc were there with him. He often thought about them, too. Thought also about Iwo Jima and all the Marines who didn't make it back and all the ones who did. He just didn't talk about it and tried to go on with his life, take it as it played out and deal with whatever came along. It wasn't always easy. But raising Jim and teaching English in the high school kept him busy full time and helped him get through the days without any contact from anyone he'd been on Iwo with or who had just been there.

Somewhere along the line, though, some old buddy had sent him a Christmas card. He couldn't remember who that was, but Jack sent cards to others. Then there was a reunion. He met some of the men from his old company. There weren't many of them. Only twelve of them had walked off the island after thirty-six days. And most of them had been wounded once or twice and sent back to the company with replacements who hadn't lasted long, either. More than a hundred of the original company had been killed. Another hundred and fifty had been wounded badly enough to be sent to a hospital ship and on to other hospitals in the Pacific and back to the States. Some of them, like Vaughn, had gotten to Saipan but died there. Others had died after the war, still casualties of the war that never left them. Arnold and some of the others he learned about later had committed suicide. He'd been a happy-go-lucky kid from Louisiana who got caught out in front of the company and got hit by a Japanese Nambu machine gun one day. For the better part of the afternoon and all through the night, he lay out in front of the company line. Jack and Roc had seen him get hit and could see him for a while the battle was still going on. After the machine gun fire had died down and the mortars came whistling in less frequently, they could no longer see Arnold and didn't know what had happened to him. Bake and Robinson wanted to go try to find him and bring him back, but Dubois said to wait until they knew where he was or they'd be lying there beside him.

"Fuckin' Japs've got caves all over this shithole where they pop out of to kill your ass."

Just at dawn the next morning, somebody spotted a man crawling slowly toward the line. Roc started to shoot him when somebody else shouted out, "It's a Marine. Don't shoot."

The man kept crawling slowly toward them, feebly lifting an arm every so often. When he got closer, Bake and Robinson sprinted out to get him and dragged him back down the hill. The man was dirty and bloody, his face swollen with sand stuck on it like glue as though it were an artist's rendition of the carnage of war. Doc Childers began checking out the wounds.

"Who in the hell is it?" Robinson asked. "He don't look like any of us."

"It's Arnold, Robbie. Your buddy from Louisiana."

"That can't be," Robinson said. "Jesus H. Christ, it don't even look like him."

"Look at the name on his dungaree jacket. That's him all right."

"Jesus Christ," Robinson said and turned away, gagging. "I can't believe it."

The litter bearers took Arnold back to the beach and left him at the division hospital. Later, somebody heard that he had lived. But nobody knew what happened to him for a long time after the war. Then Jack heard that he'd gone out into the woods and killed himself. He'd become a preacher after the war, got married and had four kids. An old company machine gunner named Wilson had found out about what had happened when he was helping put together a reunion and went to see the family. He'd written Jack in a letter that the kids were happy to see somebody who knew their daddy in the war. They wanted to know what had happened to him that made him turn out as he had afterwards. He'd been mean to them, they said, preached fire and brimstone, and they'd never seen him smile or laugh. Finally, one day he took a double-barreled shotgun and walked out into the woods. One of his sons found him two days later, lying back in the grass between two trees. He'd put both barrels in his mouth and pulled the triggers. And nobody ever knew what had happened that caused Arnold to become the way he did or why he took his own life. He never left a note or talked with anybody about his problem, his kids said.

Jack Britton had always wondered what the true Iwo Jima casualty count would be if and when the final tally were made and everybody who was Iwo blasted and had died from their wounds had been counted. Many more, he thought, like from any battle. Arnold and thousands of others like him didn't die in the battles but undoubtedly died from their personal battles years later. And in the next few years, Jack was back in touch with men he'd known, met others who'd been on Iwo Jima and learned how their lives had gone after the war was over. Most of the men who came to the reunions had lived with their experiences after some rough times and had had good lives. It was good to get together with them and talk about things, remember those who didn't make it back. It made him feel better somehow. And he began speaking about his experiences to classes at the local high school where he taught and to community groups. Then when the fiftieth anniversary of the February 19, 1945, landing on Iwo Jima rolled around in 1995, Jack had retired from teaching and gone back to the island with a group of Iwo veterans to commemorate the battle and to remember those who had died there on both sides.

But the return was bittersweet in some ways. Like many other combat veterans who had survived their battles, he'd always had the feeling that he shouldn't have left, that he was leaving people behind when he should have stayed in their place. It was good to remember those who hadn't made it and to see some of those who had, but it also brought back many painful memories. It was an emotional thing, too, for him to see the island at peace with only fading reminders of the bloody campaign that killed almost sixty-nine hundred Americans, most of them Marines, and more than twenty thousand Japanese in thirty-six days of the bloodiest fighting in the history of the Marine Corps and to remember what it had been like during the landing and afterwards. The contrast was dramatic.

Jack could hardly believe it. Iwo Jima had been returned to the Japanese in 1968 but still had an American military presence for another twenty-five years. The Association of Iwo Jima, comprised of the Japanese survivors, negotiated with U.S. officials to hold a service to remember the dead on both sides on February 19, 1985, the fortieth anniversary of the battle. Some two-hundred seventy U.S. veterans and family members flew in from Japan on military planes and came together with about one hundred Japanese representatives for the first Reunion of Honor.

By the fiftieth anniversary of the battle in 1995, the island was a Japanese military installation that could only be visited with special permission from the Japanese government. Jack and nearly eight hundred Iwo Jima veterans, their families and other interested people flew in from Guam in mid-March for the Reunion of Honor on the first commercial jet aircrafts

permitted to land on Iwo Jima. Before the planes set down on
the runway of the main airstrip at the north end of the island,
they banked sharply so everyone could see Mount Suribachi at
the southern tip of the island. Looking down on the long-dead
volcano, then north and down along the seven landing beaches
(where the Fourth and Fifth Marine Divisions had landed on
D-Day) from his window seat, Jack had the same feeling of awe
about how they'd ever gotten off the beach as he had had fifty
years before when he and Roc and Bake had hiked up to the top
and looked down after they'd been pulled off the lines for a
couple of days. The field of fire from Suribachi was tremendous.
How did they ever get off the beach? He still wondered that. It
looked almost impossible. The number of casualties undoubtedly would have been much higher initially had Lt. Gen.
Tadamichi Kuribayashi hit the landing force earlier and harder
on the beach at the outset.

The strong smell of sulphur hit Jack's nose immediately
when he walked out of the plane and down the portable exit
ramp. For just a few seconds, he expected to hear the swish-
swish-swish of an incoming mortar round or the BOOM of an
exploding artillery round coming in from somewhere off in the
flat to the south and landing right on the airstrip to hit as many
as possible. His jaw tightened as he stepped on the tarmac and
scanned the horizon. But everything looked so tranquil and
quiet that he knew the incoming he always listened for wasn't
there any more.

"Goddamn, I never thought I'd lay a foot on this island
again," somebody said.

"I never thought I'd get off the son-of-bitch," somebody
else said.

That brought a round of nervous laughter and continued

chatter as the group headed to a large hangar just off of the tarmac for a briefing of what to expect during the day on Iwo Jima. Then everybody headed out to load on trucks with active duty Marines from Okinawa who had come to Iwo Jima to transport the returning veterans around the island. The trucks would take them to an area overlooking the landing beaches for the ceremony and after that everybody could go off on their own and hitch a ride from one of the trucks that would continue to drive around the island until just before sunset when the planes would depart Iwo Jima.

On the way to the ceremony, Jack looked out at the beaches and searched for other areas he knew he'd fought through and seen men die and was struck by the change. He and the others who had fought on Iwo Jima had noted immediately that there was vegetation everywhere inland and off the beaches. With seventy-two days of pre-invasion bombardments from the big guns at sea and three more days (when ten were requested) of bombardment by a cruiser division and three battleships just before the landing, the island had looked as barren and forlorn as some alien planet when they had landed on D-Day and only got worse in the next thirty-six days. By the fiftieth anniversary of D-Day on Iwo Jima, when the island had essentially been back under Japanese control for more than twenty-five years, that had all changed. The vegetation covered the island, and it looked quite peaceful. On the fortieth anniversary of the landing on Iwo Jima, a permanent site overlooking the landing beaches for a Reunion of Honor had been selected and a monument was placed on the site. Jack had read, re-read and memorized the words on the monument soon afterwards when he'd first seen the words on an A&E documentary aired not long after the anniversary event and frequently found the words running through his mind or coming out of his mouth just like one of his favorite poems often did: *"Reunion of Honor on the Fortieth Anniversary of the Battle of Iwo Jima, American and Japanese veterans meet again on these same sands, this time in peace and friendship. We commemorate our comrades living and dead, who fought here with bravery and honor, and we pray that our sacrifices on Iwo Jima will always be remembered and never repeated. February 19, 1985, Third, Fourth, Fifth Division Associations: USMC and The Association of Iwo Jima."*

Jack Britton thought that summed things up pretty well when he first heard it. But he also knew that peace and friendship are much easier to put in words on a monument than they are to attain for those involved, on both sides, after all the killing and dying that had taken place in the battle for Iwo Jima. At the time he had wondered if forty years were enough time to have passed to forget and move on. He often wondered that through the years. Some of his old Marine buddies still harbored feelings of hostility for the Japanese and wouldn't buy anything they made and would never consider making a trip back to Iwo Jima or embracing their former enemies.

"I didn't like the bastards then," Jack could hear Roc saying, if he were still alive, "and I like them even less now. I didn't even want to go to Iwo that first time. Too damn bad I did."

Jack didn't feel that way. He was proud of his service on Iwo Jima. And while he still felt uneasy about the Japanese because of what he'd gone through, he thought the trip back to Iwo Jima and seeing the island so peaceful and serene would take away some of the hate and anger that he'd felt for the Japanese and had felt for years. He listened to the ceremony and speeches on the fiftieth anniversary and sat there wondering how the few surviving Japanese soldiers across the way felt about being there and how they thought about seeing the enemy up close that had killed more than twenty thousand of their comrades. For his own part, Jack thought of Shakespeare's King Henry's words to Westmoreland before the battle at Agincourt in 1415 and applied them to the time and to the men he'd landed with on Iwo Jima. Those words kept running through Jack's head with memories of all that happened on the little island before he was legally old enough to drink: "... *This day is call'd the feast of Crispian: He that outlives this day, and comes safe home, Will stand a tip-toe when this day is named, And rouse him at the name of Crispian. He that shall outlive this day, and see old age, Will yearly on the vigil feast his neighbours, And say, 'To-morrow is Saint Crispian:' Then will he strip his sleeve and show his scars, And say, 'These wounds I had on Crispian's day.' Old men forget; yet all shall be forgot, But he'll remember with advantages What feats he did that day: then shall our names, Familiar in their mouths as household words, — Harry the king, Bedford and Exeter, Warwick and Talbot, Salisbury and Gloster, — Be in their flowing cups freshly remember'd. This story shall the good man teach his son; And Crispian Crispian shall ne'er go by, From this day to the ending of the world, But we in it shall be remembered, — We few, we happy few, we band of brothers; For he to-day that sheds his blood with me Shall be my brother; be he ne'er so vile, This day shall gentle his condition: and gentlemen in England now a-bed Shall think themselves accurst they were not here; And hold their manhoods cheap whiles any speaks That fought with us upon Saint Crispian's day.*" No doubt that that applies to those of us who fought here, Jack thought. And we will be remembered. We are a special band of brothers. From the time at Camp Tarawa on the big island in Hawaii when we started training in earnest for taking Iwo Jima, or Workman Island as they called it, until we were aboard ship and headed west, we grew increasingly closer to one another. What had begun as a desire to fight the Japanese for our country after the attack on Pearl Harbor changed over time to fighting for one another to stay alive a day at a time, getting the war over with and getting back home in one piece.

After the ceremony was over, Jack and Iwo Jima veterans from both sides shared a few awkward moments with each other, shaking hands and bowing. With the language barrier and the uncomfortable feeling, the meeting was almost surreal to Jack. But he felt good about being there. He knew the words on the monument didn't really capture the lingering bitterness and hatred each side had for the other. Those feelings, he felt, were being papered over with the words. But the monument and the meetings were a great start on the road to reconciliation. Which he thought was never easy for meetings of old enemies, even after forty or fifty years.

"I didn't know how I was going to handle this," a man with one arm off at his shoulder and a patch over his left eye said to nobody in particular after he'd shaken hands with a former Japanese soldier. "But I feel much better now than I ever thought I would."

It was quiet after that. And as soon as the group of Americans was able to leave the area of the ceremony that overlooked the landing beaches and travel around the small island, Jack sat back quietly and thought about his route to Hill 362A where he'd been hit. He saw there on Red One Beach where Larson had died. On the top of Suribachi, Jack looked down at the spot and tried to imagine where the Nambu machine guns had been set up that provided the enfilading fire that killed Larson and so many others before the guns were silenced forever. Jack stood out on the northern edge of Suribachi and looked out over the landing beaches, all with people strolling along and pointing up over the terraces where the Marines had crawled or ran up and over to get off the beach, and then off to the west and followed his route with his eyes up the western coast and inland past Airfield Number One toward the second airfield, Nishi Ridge and Hill 362A.

He was still standing there when someone hollered to him that the truck he was on was loading up to leave. Later, the trucks passed the area where the mortar had taken Bake's head off. Jack shuddered as the pictures flashed across his mind as if it were yesterday. He could see the men all quite clearly, young and brash looking at first, then old and tired as time passed, their innocence gone forever.

On across the island where they turned north to take the airfields, he saw places where he'd seen men go down or get blown to bits. Their faces and the situations became a montage of death and destruction as one frame after another came to mind. And he could hear the swish-swish-swish of the incoming Japanese one hundred fifty millimeter howitzers and one hundred twenty millimeter mortars, exploding with a Kat-ZOON and killing anything and everybody in reach. He vividly remembered seeing an artillery round hit a man whose name he never learned, taking both legs and leaving the upper torso intact. The man sat on the edge of a shell hole, terror in his eyes. Jack stood looking out at the spot where he'd been hit and Roc had been killed. Hill 362A and Nishi Ridge were in front of him. *"For he today that sheds his blood with me Shall be my brother...."*

Rest in peace, brothers, Jack thought, and we will remember what your did here.

After he returned from the trip back to Iwo Jima, he spent more and more time during his retirement talking to community groups and students about the war and Iwo Jima and writing about his experiences and about the concerns of veterans. He wanted people to know and remember the sacrifices men long dead had made for freedom so everybody could have a better life, and he wanted everybody to know the horror of war. He didn't want those who lost their lives to be forgotten, their deaths to have been for nothing. Maybe that was the reason he'd lived, he thought, to help them be remembered. Before the country went off to war again, too, he didn't want the sacrifices of war — or the lessons learned — to be forgotten, and he talked to reporters and historians anytime they called for an interview, and he wrote a memoir primarily for his son. And he sat down for an interview for the Veterans Administration's project to preserve war experiences and talked about his time in the Marine Corps and the time he'd spent on Iwo Jima. Years of bottled-up memories and emotions poured out of Jack in that interview for posterity and helped fill the empty void he often felt when he thought of the terrible loss of life during the war.

Then because Jim hadn't been able to go to Iwo Jima with his father, he asked him to attend the World War II Memorial dedication in Washington, made all the arrangements and went along to help his father get around during the weekend events. Visiting all the sites and talking to all the people helped make it all seem worthwhile for both father and son. At the Marine Corps Memorial in Arlington Cemetery, a gunnery sergeant in dress blues walked up to them when he saw the Iwo Jima Survivor, Fifth Marine Division hat Jack was wearing and said, "You were on Iwo Jima, sir?"

"Yes, sir. All of sixteen days. Then I came home. I'd had enough of it by then."

The gunny smiled, offered his hand to Jack and said, "Thank

you very much for your service to the Marine Corps and to the country, sir. We can never thank you enough for what you and your fellow Marines did there in the name of freedom."

"Thank you, Gunny," Jack said. "That's nice of you to say. I appreciate hearing that for all of us. People sort of take what they got for granted after a while. The Corps has a great history that's part of American history. I was just telling my son about the first flag going up."

"Outstanding, sir. I'll bet that was something to see."

"I didn't actually see it go up. We were busy at the time. But we heard a rumble start out kind of low and then picked up to a loud roar when we all looked toward Suribachi after somebody shouted out, 'The flag, the flag,' and we saw Old Glory waving there against the bleak sky in the background. You could hear that roar all over the south end of the island that morning. The ships off the coast started blowing horns and whistles."

"Outstanding, outstanding."

"It was outstanding, quite a beautiful sight."

"Yes, sir, I'm sure it was," the gunny said, looking up at the memorial with the six Marines raising the flag over Jack's shoulder. "The second flag made a helluva picture, too."

"Yes, it did. A great one. But the first flag is the one that mattered to us at the time. That was the one that told us we were winning the battle. A couple of my buddies and I climbed to the top of Suribachi one morning after we'd been relieved and pulled off the lines for a day or so. We stood there by the second flag that you could see over much of the island and contemplated how we were ever able to cross the beach with so much hardware raining down on us. It was unbelievable, just unbelievable that we made it off the beach. I'll never forget that sight."

"I'm sure you won't, sir. And we won't forget what you did, either. That's what this is all about. There's the Evening Parade over at Marine Barracks at Eighth and I in D.C. tonight. General Wilson and General Barrow, both World War II veterans and former commandants, will be honored and recognized. Then this evening there's a program in honor of the Memorial Dedication and World War II Marines. Are you planning to be there?"

"Hadn't heard anything about it."

"Starts at dusk. Doors open at eighteen hundred hours. Bring your son and come by. I'll meet you and take you in."

And he did. He introduced Jack and Jim to the sergeant major and pointed out generals and colonels and several other Marine Corps World War II veterans, including a short, wiry Navaho code talker named Joe Little, who also had served on Iwo Jima. An iron-gray-colored ponytail hung down on his shoulders from a bright red pisscutter of the Marine Corps League with the eagle, globe and anchor emblem pinned on the left side of the cover. One of the ribbons on his khaki shirt was a Silver Star. While the two Iwo Jima veterans talked about where they'd been in the Marine Corps, Jack told the man how much respect he had for the code talkers and the contributions they had made to the war effort and how much it meant to the Iwo Jima campaign. The Japanese couldn't break the Navaho's language or code and never had the advantage of knowing what was coming until they actually saw it coming.

"Hard telling what might have happened if it hadn't been for you code talkers, Joe."

"It took us all to get the job done. Flamethrowers made a big difference, too."

"No doubt about that. But you guys saved a lot of Marine lives on Iwo."

The Navaho nodded and smiled. "I wish we could have saved more, Jack."

"Don't we all," Jack said, "don't we all."

"Didn't you feel strange to be fighting for the country that took it from you?" Jim asked Joe, echoing a question he'd heard someone ask after the code talker movie came out a few years earlier, and they talked about the contribution the Navaho had made to tactical communications against the Japanese, particularly on Iwo Jima, to help the country that had robbed them of their land. Jack glanced at his son quickly, hardly believing what he'd heard him ask.

"I was just proud to be a United States Marine," the Navaho said, looking straight into Jim's eyes. "It's my country, too, you know."

"It sure is," Jack said. "It sure is. That's what it was all about, Jim. Our country."

Joe Little smiled again as he and Jack and his son walked through a number of Eighth and I Marines in dress blues lined up on both sides of the walkway as the three of them followed the gunny down the walkway and to the center of the parade field where they were seated in the front row with the current commandant and the two former commandants to watch the Marine Corps Band and Drill Teams. Jack was amazed when the Silent Drill Platoon flipped M-1 rifles with fixed bayonets back and forth to each other without commands. Each man caught the rifle sharply and completed a smart shoulder arms in one swift motion.

"Now I could never do anything like that," Jack said, leaning over to his son. "I was lucky to go from right shoulder to left shoulder without screwing up."

A parade of performances continued with the music and

words saluting the sacrifices of the World War II generation and the part the Marine Corps played in winning the war in the Pacific. Jack later shook hands with so many people he couldn't remember who they were or what they said. His semi-locked fingers and stiff right hand were beginning to stay curled from shaking so many hands. When the Commandant of the Marine Corps stopped to shake hands with Jack, his hand was balled up like a fist and cramped so tight he couldn't get his fingers to open to shake hands.

"Get that hand injured on Iwo, sir?" the commandant asked when they shook hands.

"Yes, sir," Jack said. "And a couple of other things. Lost lots of my buddies, too."

"Yes, I'm sure you did," the commandant said quietly. "That was too bad. But thank God for Marines like you and your buddies. You're the salt of the Corps. Glad you made it back."

Jack nodded but couldn't say much. He'd never met and talked to a commandant of the Marine Corps before and listened quietly. But Jack wasn't always sure that he was fortunate to have made it back from the war. Sometimes it seemed like those who didn't make it were better off. It'd been over for them back then, and they didn't have to deal with living with all the memories, all the fear, all the pain, all the wounds, all the losses, all the changes in the world. And he remembered standing over Bake after he'd had his head blown off and wondering how it would be possible to leave him behind, and go on. Then Jack had sat on his helmet and cradled his head in his arms and tried to cry.

Fucking Bake, he'd thought, how can you get out of here so easy and leave me and the rest of us behind to keep on going? He smiled sadly now, wondering what Bake and Roc and the others who didn't make it would have thought of the world and all the hoopla made over the World War II Memorial and those who had fought and died when they were so young.

"Fuckin' people better appreciate it," he could hear Roc saying and felt his presence. "I'm goin' to come back and haunt their sorry asses, if they don't show some kind of appreciation for what we did. Just think of all those pretty young ladies who missed out on me. That ought to be a sin — or a crime at the very least. The ladies ought to appreciate that, for sure."

"The young ladies who missed out on you back then are old ladies now," Jack said, whispering to himself and chuckling slightly. "And they're still missing out on you, I guess. But the people here today appreciate what we did, Roc. They've been wonderful."

"They're still missing me?"

"I never said that, but I suppose they are," Jack said, laughing now. "I miss you every day. You and Bake and the rest. The people here know what we did. I feel better today than anytime since we heard the war was over. We couldn't raise too much hell there on the ward in the hospital in Oakland when they dropped the bombs and the Japs finally decided to surrender. Couldn't leave the wards. But we were happy as anything that it was all over. We knew the war was over for all of us and no more of our buddies would die like you guys did. There wasn't any big celebration when the war was over with Germany like there was when the Japs surrendered, though. We were just happy then because the troops from Europe could concentrate on Japan."

"That's one landing I wouldn't have wanted to make," he could hear Bake saying.

"You wouldn't have had to," Jack said, whispering to himself again. "But everybody kept telling us that Germany was just the first step, that the war in the Pacific might go on for a long time because the Japs wouldn't surrender. The brass wanted to keep the effort concentrated, and the politicians wanted to keep on selling war bonds. After the stiff resistance at Iwo Jima and later Okinawa and all the kamikaze pilots diving into our ships, all the generals were predicting we would take a million casualties if we had to invade Japan."

"Little slant-eyed bastards were fightin' sons-a-bitches," Roc was saying. "That sounds about right. We should've just bombed the piss out of them for six months, bombed them into oblivion and then invaded. I had all that invasion shit I wanted on Iwo."

"We did bomb them, Roc," Jack said, "and almost into oblivion, too. First with the fire bombing from the flights out of the Marianas. That's what the air corps needed Iwo for, you know. And then we bombed them with atomic bombs like nobody else had at the time. Blew the hell out of both Nagasaki and Hiroshima before the Japanese surrendered. Leveled both cities. We were happy as we could be. Everybody was. Never heard one dissenting voice about using the bomb at the time. Only later did the second guessing occur."

"Second guessing?" Roc and Bake were saying together. "What the fuck about?"

"Bombing cities with the atomic bomb and killing so many civilians. We killed a couple of hundred thousand or more and quite a few others were scarred for life. Some people didn't think that was right. Better them than us, we figured. We didn't start the war. But we finished it without losing a bunch more of our people, as we would have by invading Japan. Remember Big Al Passarelli? He told me at a reunion in Albuquerque when some group or other was whining about the atomic bombs that 'if I could pry old Harry Truman's coffin lid open, I'd kiss his bony ass for having the guts to drop those bombs and get the war over before we had to go to Japan.'"

"Truman?" Bake and Roc were saying together. "How'd he drop the bomb?"

"FDR died in April right after Iwo, and Truman took over and dropped the bombs in August before we had to hit Japan. Truman's the one Big Al was talking about."

"That sounds like Big Al," Roc was saying, laughing as he always had when he saw humor in something. "I'd have kissed FDR's bony ass myself, if he'd have dropped the bombs right off the bat if that's what would've made the bastards surrender before we got to Iwo."

"We didn't have the atomic bomb ready then. That was apparently available only after Germany surrendered. That was after I got the operation in Hawaii and was in California — the young doc who had operated on some ulnar nerve injuries at Mayo Clinic in Rochester, Minnesota, with some success wanted to operate on my arm. I was wantin' to go home, so I agreed. He'd told me the ulnar nerve would grow an inch a month for eighteen months and would be as good as new after that. Didn't work with me. My ulnar nerve didn't grow a bit, but it helped me get shipped back to Oakland."

"What the hell's an ul-nar nerve?" Roc was asking.

"It's a nerve connected to the ulna — the innermost bone of the forearm."

"And what the hell are you talkin' about it for? You were

talkin' about some new kind of bomb. Then you go off talking about this ul-nar nerve."

"That's what was damaged from that sniper's rounds I took when I got hit. But I'm talkin' about people appreciating us and about how it was when the war was over. That's what I'm trying to tell you. Trying to tell you what it was like. Some gung-ho doctor in Oahu was going to send me back to combat for the invasion of Japan with a broken wrist and ulnar injuries. Acted like he didn't know I'd lost my foot, too. Hell, I couldn't even pull a trigger, if I'd have had my foot. The bastard's assistant took pity on me and secretly wrote me orders for a real hospital at Aiea where this doc from Mayo's operated on me and sent me on to the States.

"Hadn't been there long when the war was over. There were riots and rowdy celebrations in cities around California and around the country when Japan surrendered, so we were denied liberty because they didn't want us out there in the middle of things. People already on liberty had all the fun. We were devastated that we were restricted to the hospital and couldn't go help celebrate the end of the war with Japan that we'd helped achieve. Instead, we could only read about the celebrations of others and look at the pictures in the newspaper. That was a very sad time for us, just sitting there. Some men went AWOL. I didn't, but I sure as hell wanted to be a part of that celebration and remember you guys like they're doin' here now."

"How long you think they're goin' to remember us, Britt?" Bake was saying. "I'll bet it's a different world out there, a whole different world. And we're dead meat, buddy. Remember? Blasted to hell and gone. Out of sight, out of mind. We're gone. Kaput. Who gives a shit about us? What do you know about the men who fought and died at Gettysburg during the Civil War? They got slaughtered there and who remembers them? Or even what they were fighting for? And who cares anymore? Old Robert E. Lee, other soldiers on both sides and their families probably thought about them until they were sucking their last breaths. And Lee was probably thinking about how he might have done something to change the tide of the battle like them fuckin' Japs might have done if they'd hit us hard at the beach right off. But who else cared, then or now?"

"They'll remember, Bake, they'll remember," Jack said, still whispering but all to himself now. "They've got to. They can't forget. I believe it's a little like old Abe said in his speech there at Gettysburg: *The world will little note nor long remember what we say here, but it can never forget what they did here. It is for us the living, rather to be dedicated here to the unfinished work which they who fought here have thus far so nobly advanced*' — and we've still got a helluva lot of work before us for what we so nobly advanced back there on Iwo a long time ago, looks to me like, if my buddies didn't die in vain and this country lives on ... I don't know whether it was in vain, boys, but you're right, it is a different world than it was back then ... better sometimes now, worse sometimes, too. ..."

Back then was what Jack had been hearing about for the past few days in Washington, the good times, the bad times, the sacrifices and the good that came from it all. He hadn't been sure about making the trip at first, but he'd been treated like royalty everywhere he went. Nobody had invited Jim and him to anything when they visited the World War II Memorial. But it brought tears to his eyes as he looked at the edifice there on the National Mall, halfway between the Capitol and the Lincoln Memorial with the Washington Monument in between and out to the front of the World War II Memorial that was to commemorate what he and Bake and Roc and all the rest had done to help save the country at the time. And people did remember. Young and old alike saw "Iwo Jima Survivor" on his hat and stopped him to shake hands and tell him thanks for his service. Just as they had done at the Evening Parade at Marine Barracks and on the streets of Washington. Something had taken place there after the parade that he couldn't believe was happening for just a minute. When all the hands were shaken and people started drifting away there, father and son and the code talker had lined up on the sidewalk outside to catch a taxi back to their hotel for the night. The gunnery sergeant came walking through the gathering crowd, everybody waiting for a cab, and spied the pair and the code talker and headed straight for them.

"Make a hole," the sergeant said, bellowing as if he were on the grinder at Parris Island or San Diego Recruit Depots. "Make a hole. Make a hole, people. I've got a couple of Iwo Jima Marines here that need a taxi. Come with me, Marines."

The sergeant stepped out in the street and walked out in the traffic and put his hand up to stop the first cab like a gate guard would at a Marine base anywhere in the world. He directed the cab in and opened the door for Jack and Jim. A middle-aged man stepped up to the cabby's window and handed the driver a twenty-dollar bill. The gunny opened the door to the second cab and held it open for the code talker. Another man handed a bill to the cabbie, and both taxis sped off. Jack was overwhelmed with the way he and the World War II veterans were being treated all over Washington. He hadn't quite expected the treatment to be so open and so heartfelt. Even Bake and Roc would have been impressed, he thought, if only they'd have been able to see it all.

It was more of the same on the Mall the next day for the formal dedication of the memorial. Jack hadn't seen or heard about anything like the crowd gathered on The Mall and all over the downtown Washington area and the outpouring of gratitude for the World War II veteran since the end of the war. And then that'd only been through newspapers and newsreels for him. He could hardly walk ten feet now without somebody saying, "Thank you, sir," some old Marine hollering out, "Semper Fi," or a father with a young son stopping to shake his hand and introduce his son to a living Iwo Jima veteran after they had noticed his cap. Jack was close enough to the stage to see the speakers and the past presidents and politicians of both parties who had worked together for a common cause while some of the World War II veterans the memorial honored were still around to appreciate it. It was a special occasion, one that pleased him a great deal. And he remembered when Japan surrendered how happy everybody was because all the boys would be coming home with a victory that would end the war now and for evermore and everyone would live happily ever after.

"Pretty fuckin' naïve, Britton," Jack said aloud.

Jim had also made arrangements for them to visit the amputee ward of Walter Reed Army Medical Center while they were in Washington. Jack remembered what it was like when he learned he'd lost a foot and wanted to stop by and talk with the young men and women from the Afghanistan and Iraqi wars in the same situation and tell them that losing a limb wasn't the end of the world, that life goes on regardless of what happens to a person. He'd always done that whenever he could. It wasn't long after the war that he had started stopping by the VA hospitals regularly to see the veterans there to let them know people still remembered and still cared about them. Some men didn't want visitors, but most of them welcomed somebody to stop by and talk.

An old friend from Jack's hometown had lost an arm and both legs on Okinawa at the end of World War II and called one day during the Vietnam War and wanted him to go to the Philadelphia Naval Hospital to visit men on the amputee ward. The man felt it was his duty to make visits to these men. Jack had liked the idea and went along. At the hospital, they were talking to some twenty young Marines who had just lost a leg or an arm in Vietnam about how they'd have some rough spots but they could have a good life, even with the disabilities they got in the war. Life wouldn't be exactly the same, but it wasn't over.

One baby-faced young Marine with a leg lopped off in a jagged cut just below the knee had been listening, but was frowning and fidgeting as Jack's friend talked about how he had lived a good life, had a wonderful family and got along very well with his injuries. Finally the young Marine said, "No shit, Sherlock. Some of what you're sayin' is right on. But a helluva lot you know about it all. You just lost your fuckin' arm. Try getting a leg blowed off and see how that is."

Jack laughed and said, "I did but — "

His friend smiled, waved a hand and stood up, dropping his trousers to reveal both legs off, one just below his knee and the other a few inches above the ankle. "I did and I figured I'd have to play the hand I was dealt. They said I'd never walk, but I have for more than twenty years. Had a job, raised a family and still keepin' at it."

"I-I'm sorry," the young Marine said, his face flushing. "I didn't know."

"Course you didn't know. You do now. Just don't let nothin' stop you from doin' what you want. You done your job over there, done what you was asked. Getting wounded comes with the territory, I reckon. Lots of people are worse off than you or me and get along. So can you."

At Walter Reed years later, Jack and his son were taken to see a Marine who had been wounded and lost his left arm in Iraq not quite two months earlier. His door was shut and a dozen or more snapshots of Marines on duty somewhere in Iraq were posted on the door. Scrawled across a paper under the photos was a handwritten note that said, "Do not disturb — But check at the desk first, if you must." A headline stretched across the top of the door said, "It's a Marine thing!" The Army major escorting them opened the door, stuck his head in and said, "I got a couple of old Marines out here who'd like to visit with you."

"Send 'em in," the young man said and stood from the edge of the hospital bed where he'd been sitting. He was painfully thin looking, wiry though. The left arm was off at his elbow, the right hand was still there, both heavily bandaged. He had a cast on his right leg and burns and shrapnel wounds up the inner thigh of his left leg. He had a tight smile on his face and waved at the chairs with his bandaged right hand. "So you're old Marines, huh?"

"Only one old Marine," Jack said, smiling. "This is my son, Jim. Would've made a helluva Marine, but he didn't join up. He changed his mind."

The young Marine glanced at Jim, shrugged and sat back on the edge of the bed.

"Then I got too old," Jim said.

"That about happened to me," the man said.

"So you don't want any visitors?" Jack asked. "Your door says so, anyway."

The young Marine smiled and said, "Oh, that's a Marine thing. I went to a Sting concert last night and was tired. Didn't want to be bothered. Glad to talk to you. Where were you?"

"Iwo Jima."

"Iwo Jima? No shit? You were there? That's awesome. They're giving me a Silver Star at the Iwo Jima Memorial over in Arlington next week."

"That for when you got hit?"

"Yeah."

"What happened?"

"We were out on reconnaissance patrol for a supply convoy near Fallujah in Iraq's Al-Anbar province in the middle of the afternoon a couple of months ago when we got hit. We were about halfway through the mission when we drove into the ambush, and they opened up on us with machine gun fire and RPGs — rocket propelled grenades. All hell broke loose. Driver got hit and was too stunned to keep driving. So we stopped and engaged right in the middle of the kill zone. It was some crazy shit. The Humvee was getting riddled, and the driver had been hit bad. We were right in the middle of it. Looked like we were all going to get wasted.

"Fuckin' guy on the SAW froze when we first got hit — you know what a SAW is? It's a Squad Automatic Weapon, an M249 5.56 millimeter machine gun that can lay down a helluva lot of rounds in a short period of time. I lost my left arm when the first RPG hit my weapon and exploded. I didn't feel nothin', but I saw my arm laying in the bottom of the Humvee and thought it was somebody else's at first. Fuckin' SAW would have stopped them fuckin' ragheads, if the dude firin' it would've put out some firepower. He got hit and couldn't do anything, so I grabbed the SAW out of his hand and started returning fire. I tried to raise my left arm up to help and saw that it'd been blown off about halfway between the wrist and the elbow and my bones were bare.

"Somebody tied a tourniquet around my arm and gave me a shot of morphine while I was firin' away. I kept crankin' out the rounds, and we were doin' okay when I got hit with another RPG by some other fuckin' raghead motherfucker and lost the use of my right hand. Piece of shrapnel had already caught me in the leg. Fucked it all up, shattered the femur. Radio operator got a tourniquet tied around my leg. By then we'd killed twenty or thirty of the bastards, and the other fuckin' ragheads had cut and run. They didn't want any more of the shit we were throwin' at 'em. Good thing because they could have totally destroyed the Humvee with us in it.

"You get hit on Iwo?"

"Yeah," Jack said. "Nothing like you did. Sniper got me in the hand and arm. Then I took some shrapnel in my foot and lost it to gangrene. I was lucky."

"Guess I was, too." the young Marine said and laughed. "Both of us. We're still here."

"Right."

"Fuckin' aye. And I'll be able to wipe my own ass someday."

Jack laughed, nodded and listened to the young Marine tell more about his experiences in Iraq, his second tour there, and his hospital experiences after being wounded, and Jack flashed back to fighting the Japanese on Iwo Jima and the numerous hospitals he'd spent time in along the way back home. And listening to the young Marine, Ernie Eastin came to Jack's mind almost immediately. Eastin was the bravest man in action he'd ever seen among a large number of brave men. Some people thought Eastin was just foolhardy, but he had tremendous courage under fire. Before joining the Fifth Division he'd been a Para-Marine and had made several jumps early in the war. The Para-Marines were disbanded because jumping on the islands wasn't practical, and the Marines were sent to the infantry. On Guadalcanal, Eastin had been awarded the Silver Star for rescuing an officer behind enemy lines and was always doing something beyond what was expected.

"Hey, youse guys," he had said once when everybody was talking about the latest move up. "My old man's a Chicago cop, and I want to be a Chicago cop someday. So I'd like do something to make the Chicago papers to make him proud of me and to help get on the force after the war. How 'bout we get at it and kill us some Japs today and get this war over with?"

"Ain't goin' be no 'after the war,' if you're not more careful," Roc said. "You're nuts."

Eastin had just laughed. He was always way out front of the lines. The troops moved out on a relatively even line and tried to keep it even. That was too slow for Eastin. He'd sprint out ahead of the company and take on the enemy single-handed whenever he could. Any time he'd passed dead Marines after they had hit the beach, he'd always stooped over and picked up their M-1s and grenades. So he always had two or three rifles slung over his shoulder and hand grenades hanging all over him.

Once Jack and the rest of the company close by saw Eastin winding his way toward a Japanese pillbox through a slit trench that led to it. They saw him coming and kept lobbing grenades into the trench. He'd jump out when they exploded. They'd throw one out by him, and he'd jump back into the ditch until that one exploded, all the time moving forward. Sometimes he'd grab the grenade before it exploded and throw it back at them. He got shrapnel in his leg and his jaw and kept right on going. Finally, he got to the pillbox but his rifle was empty, so he started beating Japs over the head with the butt of his rifle until the main line got there.

"Can you believe that guy?" Bake said, watching him beat the Japanese soldiers.

"Fuckin' guy's crazy," Roc said. "Ain't no other way to explain it."

Eastin and Red and Robinson and Ski and Bake and Roc and Dubois and the rest would have fit right in with the young Marine, Jack thought. Or he would have fit right in with them. Either way. Sitting there in the hospital room, Jack was taken by his observation that men from two different wars, two different eras had so much in common as young Marines. But he couldn't help but compare the differences in hospitals he'd been in when he was wounded on Iwo Jima nearly sixty years earlier to the ultra modern room the wounded young Marine from the war in Iraq was in, surrounded by all kinds of electronic devices for medical purposes and a telephone with a headset and ear phones, a CD player, radio and television and some chairs for visitors. There'd been nothing like that at the hospital on Guam or Hawaii or even in the stateside hospitals in Oakland or at Great Lakes near Chicago. Except for the different times, Jack thought being wounded probably wasn't much different now. It still hurt you, but modern medical technology and helicopter medivacs made all the difference from the time you got hit. Even with the advances of modern medicine during the war years, he figured some of the methods and technology of his war were undoubtedly closer to that of World War I than to that of the war in Iraq. People were saved in Iraq who would have died before ever getting back to the beach on Iwo Jima or headed off for a hospital far away.

"How long before you got out of there after you got hit?" Jack asked, thinking back to the tent at the Fifth Division hospital on Iwo that had been his first stop after he got hit. Nothing there but cots. Nurses there told the wounded that they were in a new tent, that mortars had destroyed the old tent the night before. Nobody wanted to stay there long. They were happy to be transferred out to the hospital ship the next day. But it had floodlights shining on the huge Red Cross on its top that was supposed to keep it safe. Not long before Jack had been wounded, they were told, a kamikaze pilot had hit one of the other hospital ships, despite the lights and Red Cross signaling a non-combatant ship. Not very comforting news all the way around.

"I guess I was back to a triage tent in less than an hour," the young Marine said. "I didn't plan on dying, but I didn't know how much longer I was going to make it when a doctor hooked me up with something and put me out for the next ten days. I was back at Bethesda by then and didn't know a thing from about an hour after I was hit until I woke up. Weird feeling."

"It's good that you're out at times," Jack said. It'd been almost a day before he had been taken aboard ship and had his wounds cleaned. He'd been put to sleep for that. Afterwards, two young corpsmen carried him back unconscious and tried to hoist him into an upper bunk, but one side of the stretcher slipped off the side of the bunk and dumped him on the floor. Jack didn't wake up, but when he did come to a couple of hours later, his jaw hurt and he had a bandage on his face. He didn't know what happened until some of the other wounded men told him he'd been dropped from a top bunk by the corpsmen. Right away the two sailors came to him and asked him not to report them. They said they didn't think he was hurt seriously and hadn't reported it. They also said that if he didn't think he was hurt seriously and wouldn't report them, they'd take care of him the rest of the way to Guam.

Jack didn't report them and the two corpsmen were at his beck and call all the way there. They shaved him, they brought him treats and they were always asking if they could do anything. Because of getting dropped on his head, the trip was almost pleasant, except that a Marine across the aisle from him died on the way to Guam. He had been moaning and screaming out in pain, making it difficult for anybody to sleep. He had stomach wounds, but many of the men told him to shut up and bear the pain the way they had to do. Jack didn't say anything because he kept thinking how much worse it would have been to have stomach wounds than on the arms and hands and feet and legs. When the man died, Jack didn't have to feel guilty about how he'd treated him, but many of the others did and hung their heads in shame for a while. They had thought the man just wanted attention. As it turned out, he needed more attention than he got.

"I got treated about as quick as it's possible to be treated under the circumstances," the young Marine said. "I'd probably have died if I'd have been hit like this back in World War II."

"Many of them did," Jack said, staring out through the window to the yard below. At the Quonset hut hospital on Guam, he had met men from his company and from the Twenty-seventh and Twenty-eighth Marines. They talked about men who had died. Major Antonio, the battalion executive officer who'd taken shrapnel in his buttocks and had to lie on his stomach all the time, was there. Jack'd talked to him and the others about their time on Iwo Jima. There was no saluting or any other officer-enlisted man relationship. It was all man to man. And Red Gallagher and Bill Bowman, who both got hit not long after he did, hollered at him when they arrived on the ward. It was Red who told him that Roc had been killed by the sniper with a single shot to the throat. Jack felt a jolt when Red told him. He'd thought that might have been the case all along but as long as he didn't know for sure, Roc was still alive in his mind. Now that he knew for sure Roc was dead, Jack couldn't trick himself any longer that his buddy was alive. *Al is gone. The sniper chose Al, right next to me. How could this be? We were three; Now there's me, Just me. Why me? Why?*

"Got Roc about the same time they got you," Red said. "He never knew what hit him."

"That's right, Britt," Bowman nodded and said. "We lost a boatload of good people on that little fuckin' rock. More 'n we ever dreamed we would. Fuckin' people who figured we could take that island in seventy-two hours didn't know what the hell they were talkin' about."

"And they didn't have to worry about being one of the lost, either," Red said.

Jack met Red years later at a reunion, but Bowman later became one of the good people that was lost along the way. Jack had thought about him a great deal through the years. He was from Jack's hometown and had been best man at his wedding. He was a man Jack thought would be okay after the war. He was a very bright, outgoing, tall and handsome man who looked much like the young Marine at Walter Reed. For some reason, though, Bowman never quite found himself after Iwo Jima. He never started college like some of his old buddies, drifted around for a couple of years doing odd jobs, sold cars for a while, then began selling insurance the last Jack knew anything about him. Even tried to sell Jack a policy while he was still in college. After he'd started teaching and Bowman had moved to California and was tending bar in Hollywood, Jack heard that he'd committed suicide, obviously another casualty of the many later casualties of Iwo Jima. Jack wondered how the young Marine they were visiting at Walter Reed would make it through the years.

At twenty-eight years old, this man was older than many of the ones Jack had known in World War II. But the young corporal was the same kind of man Jack had known nearly sixty years earlier. Men in both eras, all from a variety of backgrounds, wanted to be there and would do just about anything to get there. He'd started trying to get his parents to sign the papers so he could join the Marine Corps when he turned seventeen. With several other young men from their neighborhood they knew already in the Marine Corps and fighting in the South Pacific, they'd refused to give their permission and finally refused to talk to him about it any more.

"I want to be a Marine," young Jack had said, pleading with his mother at first. As he'd said the word Marine, he stood straighter and envisioned himself with other good men like himself, sparkling on the battlefield in dress blues, shined shoes and a chest full of ribbons. That vision always put him up on stilts. Made him feel like a million dollars. He'd seen the war movies since the attack on Pearl Harbor and wanted to help John Wayne and Ronald Reagan end the war. And he wondered how in the hell the government could have such silly regulations where a grown man of seventeen should have to ask his parents permission to do anything.

Several young men he knew had lied, forged birth certificates or somehow wiggled their way through and enlisted in one of the services even when they were younger than seventeen. But Jack's mother threatened to call the police if he tried to forge their names or somehow managed to slip through and joined up. And he couldn't figure out any way to get around having his parents' signature to enlist without forging them. Larson said he didn't have to forge his parents' signature. He had found his original birth certificate when he was fifteen and saw that it didn't have the year of birth written in the space for the date or any other year on the paper. So he wrote in 1925 instead of 1928 and shipped out while he was still fifteen.

"I wanted to join the Marine Corps since I can remember," the young Marine at Walter Reed said, still sitting on the edge of his hospital bed. "And I want to stay in. I didn't go through all this shit in Iraq and all the trouble I went through to get in the Corps to get out now."

"Not much chance of that, is there?" Jack asked.

"I hope so. I can't let that SAW fuckin' rip like I used to, but there's a lot of things I'll be able to do for the Marine Corps. They're goin' to give me a claw, then a hand that I can grasp things with." He smiled again and said, "When I can grab hold of some chow, I'll be almost as good as new. My girlfriend from North Carolina is coming up next weekend. She's goin' have to do the grabbin' some things 'til I get my claw and the other hand heals, if you know what I mean. I'm looking forward to that."

"You've got the attitude," Jack said, laughing. "That's half the battle."

Jim told about seeing a television program about a soldier who'd lost a leg in Iraq a year ago and was back in combat training with a high-tech prosthesis that didn't seem to slow him down or make him any less capable. The soldier was shown on TV participating in some kind of hand-to-hand combat exercise and was holding his own, passing all strength and endurance tests, Jim said.

"That would never have happened in my time," Jack said, holding up his hand. "'Course we didn't have all the high-tech things they've got today. You lost a limb back then or got something like you've got and you were gone. One old doc did try to send me back to combat before he saw I'd lost a foot, too. Wouldn't have made any difference, if he hadn't. I couldn't even have pulled the trigger with my hand and fingers the way they were, the way they are."

"It's not that way now, like your son says," the young Marine said, then told about how much of a battle it had been for him to join the Marine Corps. He said his parents had divorced when he was young, and he'd bounced back and forth between them, never doing well in school and getting into more and more trouble as he grew into his teen-age years. Finally, he was arrested for robbing a convenience store and sent to youth camp for juvenile offenders. He served twenty-three months and got out and could find nothing but a job in a pizza joint. He tried to join the Marine Corps but was told that it'd never happen with his background. For the next three years, he delivered or made pizzas and went to a junior college part-time and kept talking to the Marine recruiters. The paperwork was filled out and ready, if anything ever changed so he could be accepted. One of the recruiters took him on as a special project and tried every way he could think of to get the young man accepted for enlistment. Finally, the recruiter called one evening and told him he had a spot for him if he could be ready in an hour and would be by to get him.

"'I was ready yesterday, sergeant,'" the young Marine said he'd told the recruiter and hung up his apron and went by a friend's apartment he'd been living with and told him he was leaving in thirty minutes. "The rest is history. I was twenty-five years old and hadn't had a great life growing up, didn't have much of a future and wanted to be a part of something as outstanding as the Marine Corps, part of the history and tradition that you helped make. And I'd like to be able to be a part of it in the future, too. There's not any other place I'd rather spend my life. I love the Marine Corps. It's an outstanding outfit. You know that, and I'd be honored if you could come over to the Marine Corps Memorial Tuesday for the ceremony."

"I'd like to — I really would — but we're flying home tomorrow. We just came for the dedication and catch a flight back home on Sunday morning."

"Where's home?"

"Indiana."

"Mine's here right now, then wherever the Marine Corps sends me."

"Mine's Indiana now. I settled down there after the war and the Marine Corps sending me where they wanted to send me for a couple of years. Tried Florida for a while after I retired, but Indiana is home. Wish I could come Tuesday. Sounds like a great day for you."

"It will be. Wish some of my buddies could be here. Two of them got killed when I got hit, and the rest of them are still over there fightin' them fuckin' ragheads. I'd rather still be with them. That's home. Just like the Marine Corps is. We were tight. They were my Marines."

"I'm sure they were. And always will be. That's the way it is, though. We'll be thinking of you Tuesday. But we're going to have to move along before then. Going to have to move along now and see some other people, too. Let you get some rest after that concert. You probably need that."

"Semper Fi. I'll do that. Thanks for stoppin' by."

"My pleasure," Jack said, fighting back a tear. "Semper Fi. And best of luck with stayin' in the Marine Corps. They'd be losing a damn good Marine, if you have to get out."

"Thank you, sir."

Jack felt a flood of anger sweep over him as he left the hospital. He felt angry that so many young people like the young Marine were losing their lives and their limbs in the war. As angry as he was, though, and as sad as the young Marine's condition and some of the other wounded veterans from Iraq they had met were, particularly a young female soldier with a leg off above the knee from shrapnel, the visit had made Jack's trip to Washington more satisfying for being able to visit for a while with soldiers and Marines who had lost limbs and the innocence of their youth. He'd come full circle from the days of his own youth when he was on the receiving end of the incoming rounds he still heard all the time. He didn't like the wars in Afghanistan or Iraq any better than he liked any war, but his heart still went out to the young men and women he'd met who had served at one place or the other. They'd renewed his faith in the country's youth. And he wanted to show his support for active-duty members of the country's military just as much as he wanted to show his remembrance of his generation's servicemen and women.

Before heading home to Indiana, he came across another opportunity for showing that remembrance on another trip. He met a group of veterans from several theaters of the war and agreed to join them in the fall on a veteran's tour of the European battlefields of World War II and the cemeteries where many of those who were killed in the war were buried. By the time he left for Europe, his health was beginning to fail noticeably. Despite open-heart surgery a few years earlier, his heart was weak, his blood pressure was high and his physical energy at an all-time low. Because of his condition, Jack's doctor had advised him not to go at that time.

"When am I going to go, Doc?" Jack had asked. "There's no time like the present."

"You need to get stronger and in better health, first," the doctor had said. "It's a noble thing you want to do, but you need to be able to do it."

"What am I going to do, Doc? Die over there?"

"You could."

"I could die here, too, I'm sure. The reaper is closing in on me, my friend."

The doctor nodded and after some further discussion of medicines to take and what to do if and when emergencies came up, he agreed that Jack should go ahead and make the trip, if he thought he could, that staying home might prolong his life but wouldn't help in the long run. So Jack went to Europe and returned nearly a month before he ended up in the emergency room. He knew he might die on the trip, just as he had known he might die on his first trip to Iwo Jima.

"Might have died either place," the old man said in a whisper.

"What's that?" Jim asked, standing beside his father's bed.

"Might have died either place."

"Either place?"

"Yeah, might've died in either place. Iwo or Europe. Helluva lot of good men died in both places. I was thinkin' about the trip to Europe and what it all meant."

"You had a good time over there, didn't you?"

"We don't go to these places to have a good time," Jack said hoarsely. "We go to remember all those who died for our country so the rest of us can live free. They shouldn't be forgotten, they won't be forgotten, they can't be forgotten."

"And they won't be, Dad," Jim said, watching his father drop off to sleep.

It was a fitful, dream-filled sleep. The old man tossed and turned and moaned.

"We come here on holiday every year," the man said, one of a group of rowdy construction workers from Suffolk, England, down in a Caen, France, hotel bar where Jack and a D-Day veteran on the tour were having a drink one evening after spending the past three days along the Normandy Coast where the Allied Forces came ashore on June 6, 1944. "We come to pay our respect to the boys who didn't come home. They don't give a shit about that here."

They were men in their forties and fifties, work-hardened, rough around the edges and looking like they'd just come in off of the job for a few drinks. They'd had several by the time Jack and the other man got to the bar and were on their way to getting rip-roaring drunk, it appeared. They started talking to Jack and his friend right away, laughing with them and arguing incessantly with the bartender and the waiter over the charge for drinks they'd put on a tab they were paying. The Brits all thought they were being overcharged because they were English.

"They don't like us," another of the men said, "and we don't like them. The frogs, they're bloody bah-stards. We've come over here and saved their arses twice in the last hundred years, left a lot of our boys buried here in the process, but the frogs don't like us. They think they're better than us, better than you. And you Americans saved their arses, too, and they don't like you, either."

"Wasn't always that way," the D-Day veteran said. "They liked us plenty when we started pushing the Germans back to the east. They'd been occupied by the Krauts for so long by the time we got here that they didn't know which end was up or which way to turn. They were still afraid of the Germans but happy to see us and were soon singing a different tune. When we got to Paris and the Germans were on the run, it was party time like you wouldn't believe."

"You blokes were here during the last war?" another asked as the four crowded around the two old men. "You actually helped save these bloody bah-stards?"

"I didn't," Jack said. "I was in the Pacific. But Don was here for the duration."

"Yeah, I was here, in the Army," the D-Day veteran said. "The Big Red One. Went in on Omaha on D-Day and from there to St. Lo to Paris to the Bulge and punched through the Siegfried Line and was there for the whole shebang to the end of the war. I'll never forget the reception we got in Paris, though. The Twenty-eighth Division even marched right down the *Champs Elysees* up to the *Arc de Triomphe* before they went back into battle. The streets were lined with people — men shoving a bottle of wine or liquor in our hands, women kissing everybody and old women blowing kisses at us for freeing them."

"They were bloody well glad to see you then. The bloody, ungrateful bah-stards."

"What did you do in Paris besides go through?" another of the men asked.

"We stayed half-crocked for two days," he said, laughing. "Then we moved out again."

That called for another round of drinks and a toast.

"And where were you in the Pacific?" the older man of the group asked Jack.

"Iwo Jima," he said.

"Iwo Jima?" two of the men said at once. "That was a very bloody, well-known battle."

"Yes, it was quite bloody."

"I was in your country a few years ago," the older man said. "And I saw the Iwo Jima statue at Arlington Cemetery near where me sister lives. Quite impressive. And you were there?"

"On Iwo? Yes, for a few days."

"Hear, hear," another of them said, raising his glass again. "Give these men another drink. This one helped save your arse, and this one was on Iwo Jima fightin' the Nips. They're boys after me own heart. And they're here to remember the boys who didn't come back, too. Just like we are. To remember those who saved your arses and lay buried in your fields."

"'*In Flanders Field*,' lads," the fourth man said and the others joined in, "'*the poppies blow Between the crosses row on row, That mark our place; and in the sky The larks, still bravely singing, fly Scarce heard amid the guns below. We are the Dead. Short days ago We lived, felt dawn, saw sunset glow, Loved and were loved, and now we lie In Flanders fields. Take up our quarrel with the foe: To you from failing hands we throw The*

*torch; be yours to hold it high. If ye break faith with us who die We shall not
sleep, though poppies grow In Flanders fields.'*

"'*If ye break faith with us who die We shall not sleep, though poppies
grow in Flanders fields,*'" the old man went on, reciting the last line
of one of his favorite poems as he woke again in the hospital in
late afternoon. "And we shall not be forgotten."

He was surrounded by more people he didn't recognize, that
he was sure he'd never seen before. Two of them were young,
dark-skinned, foreign-looking people in white coats. For a
minute he thought they were Japanese, and his heart rate nearly
doubled on the monitor off to the side of the bed and above his
head. He really had been captured. But it wasn't a Japanese voice
he heard. Something else. More British than American. And
another Negro man. Dubois and Robinson would have something to say about that. They were always calling Negroes
"niggers" or "niggra" or "coloreds" at best and didn't like them
one bit, said they were dirty and lazy and couldn't be trusted
and couldn't "pack their gear." Dubois even told about being in
the hospital back in the states after he'd been wounded on
Guadalcanal and a light-skinned nurse who looked like she
was "colored" to him was going to give him a shot. "Huhn't
uh, no niggra is goin' to come at me with a needle," Dubois
said he'd said. "No way in hell." And she didn't, he said.
Wasn't anybody going to talk him into that. No amount of
talking about the subject changed anything. That's just the
way it was. Talking, talking, talking. Everybody was always
talking about something, not doing much about anything. And
nothing ever changed much. Somebody somewhere was talking about somebody's blood pressure being extremely high,
stroke-level high, lungs crackling, heart pumping hard and fluid
building up. Jack's head was throbbing, and he felt nauseous,

ached all through his body. Bake and Roc and the two Cajuns, Dubois and Robinson, floated above him. Childers the corpsman and Wilson the machine gunner stood off to the side, one of them poking a tube up through his nose and down through his throat to his stomach. What the hell were they doing? What the hell's going on?

"Blood down there," somebody said. "We'll have to suction it out, if there's much."

Jack's hand went to his nose and felt something taped there. He felt along the plastic covering and decided he'd been hit in the nose, too, and started to drift off to sleep again just when he heard his son's voice, "You look like Pinocchio, Dad. Your nose grew somehow since I saw you awhile ago."

"Somebody else's nose is goin' to grow," Jack said weakly, struggling to sit up and pulling at the tubes in his nose. "What the hell's goin' on here? Are they tryin' to kill me?"

"Nobody's tryin' to kill you, Dad. Lay back there and relax."

Jim, closing in on sixty years old now, stood beside the bed in the intensive care unit and looked down at his father, an old man now. They'd been together since a few years after the war when Jim had been born and his mother had died in childbirth from toxemia, something "doctors didn't know much about in those days," his father had told him years before. Even years later, the doctors only seemed to know that it brought on sudden high blood pressure, headaches and other disturbances in the body in women in the latter stages of pregnancy and sometimes brought death to the mother, as it did to Jim's mother, and allowed the baby to live, as it did him. He and his father had had some rough times since then, none rougher than the arguments they had in the first days of the Vietnam War when Jim had wanted to drop out of school and join the Marine Corps to the later days of the war when he had marched in war protests while he was off to college and swore he'd go to Canada if he got drafted.

"I don't like the goddamn war for one thing," Jack said during the first phase in one of their heated discussions about Jim's future. "I don't like any goddamn war and particularly don't like it down there in Southeast Asia where even MacArthur said we can't win a ground war. And I don't want to see you go off and die down there for nothing in a no-win situation."

"We can whip 'em in six months, and you know that, Dad. Just like we did the Japanese."

"Just like we did the Japanese, huh? We were there a helluva lot longer than six months, for one thing. And if it hadn't been for the atomic bomb, for another, we'd have been there a helluva lot longer and there'd have been a helluva lot fewer of us who made it back. They were fightin' sonsabitches. And I expect the Vietnamese are, too."

"But I want to go to see what it's like to be in combat, see what it's like to be in a war — like you did."

"That's about the most goddamn idiotic thing I've ever heard anyone say. In my whole goddamn life. You don't know what the hell you're talkin' about. Combat in any war is a totally different world. A totally different world. Completely different from anything you'll ever do. Hard and fast rules to live and die by. And it's not anything you'd ever want to do again unless you absolutely have to, if you live. And maybe you and a lot of your buddies won't live. The best buddies you'll ever have anywhere. So forget that. You understand what I'm sayin'?"

"Sir, yes, sir," Jim said, snapping a sharp salute.

"Now don't get smart. I didn't and don't always agree

with Dugout Doug MacArthur, the dogface son-of-a-bitch — he left a bunch of Americans to die in the Philippines when he left saying, 'I shall return.' Japs overran and captured the remnants of a Marine battalion and kept them in Malinta Tunnel on Corregidor 'til they died from starvation, disease and their wounds. Nearly half of them died in that damn tunnel. Well, a couple of years later, MacArthur did return to the Philippines — with the help of God and a few Marines, he returned.

"But he later said we can't win a ground war in Southeast Asia, too, and he's right about that. Those people down there will fight like hell for their home just like we would, and have, here. We need to take care of business here at home, anyway. Lots of things to do here."

"Didn't you want to get over there in the Pacific and fight the Japanese back there in your war? Didn't you join up? Couldn't wait to fight them, you told me."

"Yeah. Hell yes, I did. Different story, though. They attacked us. Everybody was joining up. We were at war, not trying to impose our way of life on another country and save everybody from communism. I couldn't wait to get in the war and get at them — until about fifteen seconds after I hit the beach on Iwo. Then I wondered what the hell I'd got myself into. It's not something you do unless you absolutely have to. Take my word for it. You won't like it. Read a book, see a movie, go camping or do anything else to satisfy your curiosity. But don't do anything stupid that'll get your dumb ass killed for nothing. You stay dead for a long time."

"That's what I've heard."

"Don't get smart with me, I said. You still put your feet under my table."

So Jim reluctantly agreed to finish high school and then went off to the university to study art. By that time, he told his father he'd changed his mind about joining the Marine Corps and going off to war. And after he was on campus for a while, he started protesting the war at rallies and marches. During the vicious fighting of the Tet Offensive early in '68, Jim and several other students had gotten arrested when the protest turned ugly and people started throwing things. The police brought out billy clubs and started swinging and arresting people. Jack saw his son on the evening news and drove the hundred miles to the university to get him out of jail. Jim had already made bail and was back on campus when Jack found him.

"What the hell is going on here, son?" Jack asked immediately. "I saw you on TV with a bunch of these fuckin' hippies. You all made the goddamn news when you got arrested."

"Sorry about that, Pop."

"You sure sound like it. I'd have let you sit in that jailhouse, but I drove down here to get you out this time and to tell you one thing: This is a free country; you have freedom of speech and a boatload of other freedoms that lots of people around the world don't have. A lot of my buddies died for what you take for granted. We're not a perfect country. No question about that. But there's always a line to get into this country. Always will be. You don't see that in any of these other countries, do you? Hell no, you don't. They're knocking down doors to get out and standing in line to get in here. And you sure as hell don't see a line of people knocking down doors trying to get out of this country, do you? Hell no, you don't. And you know why? You can think and act as you goddamn please here, within the law, and you can protest laws you think unjust. That's our system. With that freedom comes responsibility about how to live free. I still don't like the goddamn Vietnam War, but I don't like all this protest bullshit, either. I don't like the way the troops are being treated. You do what you think is right, but keep your ass out of jail and off the fuckin' television and don't let what you're doing hurt the young men over there fighting and dying. That's bullshit. Take the high road, for Christ's sake."

And that's what Jack had tried to do with his son all along. They had resolved their differences long ago and were quite close in later years. Both were loners and kept to themselves much of the time. But taking the high road hadn't always been the easiest thing for Jack to do in his personal life. He'd never re- married for reasons he had never told anybody and had raised his son alone with help from both sets of grandparents, one that lived close by on a farm and the other one in a nearby little town. And they all worked together to see that Jim had the best time growing up he could after losing his mother. Some- body was always there for him. But sometimes Jack would get quietly drunk and be pretty distant. Morose almost, with a blank stare or a faraway look in his eyes. Either way, he was some place else. Sometimes he'd start spouting poetry as though he were teaching one of his English classes or was back in time on a Shakespearean stage: "... *Life's but a walking shadow, a poor player That struts and frets his hour upon the stage, and then is heard no more; it is a tale told by an idiot, full of sound and fury, Signifying nothing. ...*" And he'd trail off and stare blankly ahead for a while. Or he'd go on, line after line, until he felt drained of emotion and empty throughout. Those times passed in a day or two and became less frequent as time went on. He still quoted poetry at the drop of a hat, but he put the bottle away for the most part and didn't drink much most of the time. He felt a little awk- ward as a father, not having a wife around to be a mother to the boy. But he'd pretty well decided he couldn't take another wife, not with the way he was crippled up. Betty had been there before and had been there after he was wounded. She understood how he felt about his wounds and treated him no differently. Others didn't understand at all and found them repulsive.

The one time Jack had tried to see another woman a couple of years after Betty's death didn't turn out well. It was the summer after he was out of college, getting ready to start teaching at the local high school. The woman was in town visiting relatives and was introduced to Jack. They met for coffee once, then went to a movie. Later they sat on the porch at her relatives' house and talked. He reached out to put his arm around her. She stiffened.

"What's the matter?" he asked.

"Oh, nothing, nothing at all."

"I don't believe that. Something's wrong. What is it?

"That hand, uh, your hand, it gives me the heebie jeebies," she said quietly. "I'm sorry. I can't help it. I don't want you to touch me with it."

"I've got a leg off, too," Jack said just as quietly. "Want to see it? It's just a fuckin' stub. Got a hole in my shoulder, too. Want to feel it? Stick your finger in the hole?"

"Oh, please," the woman said. "I'm sorry. I can't help it."

"Yeah, you are sorry," Jack said as he left. "No doubt about that. One sorry individual."

No high road there, and for the next couple of weeks, he hit the bars pretty regularly and left young Jim with his parents while he tried to get his head together and get ready for the coming school year. Mostly he just sat at a roadside bar several miles away from home, drinking alone until he felt drunk enough to go to sleep and then he'd take a six pack of Sterling beer with him just to make sure. One night a woman well into her cups in her mid- to late-twenties but looking older sat down on his left side. He stared at the back bar and took a drink of his beer.

"What're you doin' here drinkin' all alone, big boy?" she said. "Handsome feller like you ought to be out gettin' some lovin'. Bet you have to beat 'em off with a stick."

Jack didn't have a stick, so he ignored the woman at first. But she kept talking and talking, and the two of them kept drinking and drinking. After several more beers, he loosened up enough to answer her with a "yes" or a "no" or an "uh-huh." And by closing time, he was ready to do more than talk. He hadn't been with a woman for more than two years and felt the urge.

"Want to give me a ride, big boy?"

"Sure," he said, draining the last dregs of his beer and snuffing out a cigarette. " I'll give you a ride. Let's go."

Once they were in her little bungalow, they headed straight for her dark bedroom and fell together on the bed. Without lights and with no urging from the other, they undressed and got right down to business. Jack performed like a wild animal, hunching and moaning as he sought to satisfy himself. The woman was no less hungry as she arched herself up to meet him and cried out with an animal-like scream each time Jack thrust himself inside her.

Afterward, they lay panting, smoking and talking.

"You're not bad in bed, big boy," she said, taking a long drag on her cigarette. "Don't have much to be proud of as far as size goes, but you're pretty good with what you've got."

"How 'bout this for size?" Jack asked, turning on the bedside light and crossing his right leg over his left knee. "Maybe I could get this in there, and it'd feel bigger than my cock."

"My god, you're a cripple," she said, sitting up on the side of the bed and grabbing the sheet to pull around her. "Oh, my god, I fucked a cripple. A one-legged man. I fucked a one-legged man and didn't even know it. What were you, a soldier?"

"Hell no, I wasn't a soldier. I was born this way. Deformed at birth like the Hunchback of Notre Dame. I'm twisted and deformed. Look at this hand." He held it up and said, "See this twisted hand, this *'bloody and invisible hand,'* that will *'Cancel and tear to pieces that great bond Which keeps me pale! Light thickens, and the crow Makes wing to the rooky wood.'* That's *'Macbeth,'* Act Three, Scene Two, lines forty-three through forty-six. Ain't you impressed that I know Shakespeare?"

"You're crazy," the woman said, pulling the sheet tighter. "Crazy as a goddamn loon."

"Sanity ain't all it's cracked up to be, sweetheart," Jack said, putting his foot and leg back on and pulling on his pants. "Man is certainly crazy, my dear. Why else would we treat one another the way we do? Fight each other? Kill with pride? Why would we drink ourselves into a stupor and wallow around fuckin' each other like a couple of animals in heat like we just did?"

"Get your clothes on and get out of here, you crazy bastard."

"I'm gone, sweetheart. I'm gettin' out of here as fast as I can. Which ain't fast enough."

"My fiancé was killed in North Africa, and I can't stand to be around soldiers."

"Crippled ones anyway, huh? I told you I wasn't no fuckin' soldier, lady. I was born all fucked up. You ought to see some of my Marine buddies, though. Heads blowed off and split wide open like a fuckin' watermelon and guts spillin' out like you wouldn't believe, arms and legs ripped off and strung around all over the place. They're not just crippled, they're dead. Deader 'n a fuckin' doornail. Just like your fiancé. God rest his soul, lady. He's lucky he didn't make it back and have to live with you for the rest of his goddamn life."

"Get out of here, you crazy bastard," she said, keeping the draped sheet around her with one hand and holding the door open with the other. "You're lucky I don't call the police on you."

"Call 'em sweetheart. What are you goin' to tell them? That you fucked a one-legged man and didn't know it? Think they'll arrest me for that?"

"Just go, you crazy bastard."

He went and drank the six-pack of beer he'd bought before going home and fell into bed, drunker than usual and ready for sleep. The next morning he woke up with a splitting headache and decided he could live without the drinking every day and night. And after that, he decided he'd never see another woman and would never remarry, and he didn't drink, except at times when life got so overwhelming he'd go off and get quietly drunk. He worked at being a good teacher and father and spent as much time as possible with his son.

As the boy grew, Jack sometimes felt more like he was an older brother than a father. The two of them came to accept whatever the other did as long as whatever it was didn't step on the other's toes. They lived in the little farm house next to where his father grew up and in the house his great-grandmother had lived until the boy was graduated from high school when he was just seventeen, then went off to work for the summer on a road construction crew. Growing up on the farm made that a natural place for him to start working with tools. He had learned to do whatever had to be done by doing it and could run any kind of equipment or do any job.

In their years together, Jack didn't so much as try to teach his son to do anything or tell him anything about living. That wasn't his way out there, away from the classroom where he taught high school English. That was a more structured kind of learning. On the farm, he'd tell the boy what he wanted and then just expect that it'd be done. He thought that was the best way of learning in some situations. You watched, you listened and you figured it out. Simple as that. Sometimes it was a bit hard on the boy in the process, particularly when his ability level was stretched. Like when the boy started learning to play baseball and tossing one back and forth, playing catch with an older girl down the road. He was getting the hang of it. Then, one day Jack threw his ten-year-old son a new glove and a new baseball and told him they were going to play catch to break them in. Sixty feet away, Jack threw the first time, a half-speed, sidearm pitch that snapped into the kid's glove as he stuck it out defensively. He held onto the ball.

"Now, pay attention," Jack said, gripping the ball in his left hand. "I'm going to take a few warm-up tosses, then start throwing some ins and outs a little harder. Catch 'em in the web of your glove like you just did. Just don't throw 'em back before I get my glove on."

After a few harder pitches that tailed in or out at the last second and he didn't catch them in the web of the glove, Jim's hand was puffed from catching the pitches in the palm of the hand or the end of his fingers. Tears streamed down his cheeks as he went to chase a pitch he'd missed. On the way, he folded a large red handkerchief and put it inside the glove to shield his hand a little. But he didn't say a word. He just kept watching his father give a low kick and fire the ball in with his good left arm, then scoop the glove up with his left hand for the throw back.

"I threw 'em in there too hard for that little feller, didn't I?" the old man said. He opened his eyes and focused on Jim as the sun was slipping over the horizon outside the hospital window and darkness was setting in. "Remember that? Remember when I got you that new ball and glove and started pitching to you? I wanted to see if I could still throw hard."

"You could," Jim said, standing at the side of the bed, smiling. "Wish you could throw that hard now, you old fucker, and I'd catch every damn one you could sling at me."

"I 'magine you would," the old man said, murmuring. "In your dreams. That wasn't very good of me, though, was it? Pitchin' to you like you were a grown man. I wanted to see if I could throw as hard as I used to, and I just wanted to toughen you up and help you get by. Life's not always easy. But I wasn't always a hardass on you, was I? I tried to do good by you. Remember when I ran over your first cat when your grandpa was there one day?"

Jim nodded.

"And he said he'd bury her?"

"Allie? Yeah, I remember her. She was that crazy Siamese you got me for Christmas."

"Your grandpa threw her out down in the bottoms. Didn't bury her at all."

"You don't have to tell me things like that. They don't matter."

"Yeah, they do. I want to get some things straight with you: Remember when you'd have those kittens that'd come up missing and you'd say they just ran away and went some place else?

I don't know what happened to all of them, but I gave a couple of them away because we had too many. But running over that little kitten when you were just a kid and you cried and cried, that bothered me. I don't know. I never liked to kill anything, but that little dickens couldn't learn to stay out of the way until it was too late. Same thing with that old dog you liked so well.

"Old Ben Anderson came along and hit him one morning. Ran right over him then. Old Skipper would run after his car every time it came down the road and not bother anyone else's car or truck. Don't know what there was about Ben. But Skipper always knew Ben's car and would chase after it, barking like he wanted to take a bite out of it. Old Skipper died an hour or two after he got run over, and I didn't have the heart to say anything to you. Took him off and buried him before you got home that day. When he didn't show up for a day or two, I pretended he had run off like he used to for a couple of days at a time when he was out chasing around."

"I know you pretty well, old man," Jim said, grinning but with tears beginning to fill his eyes. "Think I didn't know all those things? I always wondered about Skipper, though, and wished I could've helped bury him. I knew something had happened to him. He'd never stay away for more than a day or two. Never did. He was a good old dog. Helped me through a lot of days when I needed some help. Took me awhile, but I finally figured you out somewhere along the line: That you tried to protect me from some of life's bad hands. At first, I thought it wasn't right, but when I thought about all the tough hands you'd been dealt, I went along and knew you were doing what you thought was right, what you had to do. Which is all that matters."

The old man smiled weakly and dropped off to sleep again,

thinking about dogs and cats and baseball. It was baseball that invaded his mind and captured his dreams. After the operation on his hand wasn't successful, Jack had requested to be transferred to the Great Lakes Naval Hospital in Chicago in the late summer of 1945 so he'd be closer to home. The transfer was granted, and he was happy to be within a hundred miles of home and able to follow baseball and the Cubs as he had before he joined the Marine Corps and had all the way back to his childhood days in the early Thirties. Being a Cubs fan was particularly good for him that fall because the Cubs and the Detroit Tigers were playing in the World Series. And it was even better since the Cubs' front office had sent over a large number of tickets for wounded veterans in the hospital. Jack'd never seen a World Series game and didn't even remember when the Cubs had been in a series. But he and many other wounded men were looking forward to getting to see a game and truly appreciated the Cubs organization for its gesture to the veterans. That was in the days just before the Billy-Goat Curse came down on the heads of all Chicago Cubs after somebody wouldn't allow avid Cubs fan, Greek immigrant and Billy Goat Tavern owner William "Billy Goat" Sianis to bring his pet goat Murphy along with him to Wrigley Field for the fourth game in the series. As he and the goat were being denied entrance, Sianis reportedly raised his hands in the air and put the curse on, saying, "The Cubs, they not gonna win any more. They never gonna be another World Series played at Wrigley Field." Jack didn't know about the curse at the time, but the Tigers won the fourth game 4-1 and the fifth game 8-4. The Cubs bounced back to win the sixth game 8-7 to tie the series at three games apiece to set the stage for the seventh and deciding game of the '45 World Series. But Jack and many of the wounded men never got to see any of the games because they'd refused to do what was asked of them to get one of the tickets.

The naval hospital had an overflow of patients and never had enough help. The wounded men coming back from overseas were the first priority; maintenance and cleaning in some areas often took a back seat or just never got done. Hallway and ward floors were swept and swabbed once a week and kept fairly clean. But the baseboards had an accumulated crud that had to be scraped off. The bulkheads were splattered and stained from years of use without much cleaning or painting. So there was work to be done. And there were more Marines and sailors than there were tickets to the World Series. Hospital officials announced that the Cubs had provided the tickets but there would have to be some work performed by those who received the tickets in order to earn them. Men wanting to attend a World Series game were assigned to get down on the floor of the corridors and scrape crud from the baseboards, clean the heads and a number of other dirty, rotten jobs that did need to be done but that had been long neglected or had been assigned to the regular maintenance details that were understaffed and overworked. Some men were on crutches, Jack's arm was in a cast and he'd lost his foot after the gangrene had set in and later had to have more of the leg amputated to accommodate the artificial leg. Others were much worse off. As a result of the requirement and their conditions, many of the men said to hell with going to the World Series and didn't go to any of the games. The Cubs were always at .500 or better, Jack figured, and the Cubs fans among the men were sure there would be many World Series in their future now that they'd made it back home. And Jack thought he'd be able to easily get back to Chicago for the series anytime. He lived so close, that was a foregone conclusion. Like Jack, most of the wounded Cubs fans un-doubtedly never knew about the curse of the billy-goat and probably wouldn't have believed in it had they known.

The old man came awake again, smiled slightly and shook his head. What a deal, he thought. It's been almost sixty years now, and the Cubs haven't played in a World Series in all that time. With all the good teams and good players they've had in that time, how could that be possible? That damned Billy-Goat Curse? Could that be possible? he wondered. The Cubs hadn't played in a series since then. They hadn't had a great team in '45, but they'd won the pennant and had a chance of winning the series. Most of the good players from other teams were still in the service at the time of the series that fall, and the Cubs had won the pennant with a weak lineup. And they'd started the series off winning. But it wasn't good news for the Cubs that Hank Greenberg, a great hitter, got back in time to play for Detroit. It seemed that he was always on third base or hit-ting home runs. The Cubs had no one like him back from the war. They did have some great pitching in Claude Passeau and Hank Borowy. Hank had won ten games with the Yankees and eleven more with the Cubs when he came over in July. He had won the first and sixth games in the '45 series, and had pitched five innings in the fifth game. And Charlie Grimm, the Cubs manager, decided to pitch him in the final game, but he couldn't handle four games in one series. The Cubs lost the game 9-3 and the series. They went down the drain then and have been going down ever since, Jack thought.

"Tigers couldn't hit me like they hit Borowy that day," the old man said under his breath, smiling again. He could still smile about it and often did. Many times since that '45 World Series, though, he wished he hadn't been so rebellious when he returned from Iwo Jima and had just gotten down on hands and knees and scrubbed some crud with one hand. Not many people get to see a World Series in person. He'd had his only chance to see his favorite team in one and blew it. That was life. But he still hadn't forgiven the naval hospital for the insult to wounded veterans by making them go on work details to get what the Cubs had provided for the veterans as a way of showing appreciation to them for their service and their sacrifices.

"Bastards," the old man said, murmuring the word harshly. "I'll never forgive them."

"Never forgive who?" Jim asked, coming awake himself.

"Fuckin' people who run the naval hospital."

"What have they done?"

"Why, they wanted us to scrub the floors and clean the bulkheads and all kinds of other shit before we could go to the World Series. Dirty bastards. The Cubs gave the tickets to us. Not the Navy. But they gave us the old GI shaft."

"Oh, I see what you're talking about now," Jim said, having heard the story before.

The duty nurse looked in and motioned to Jim to follow her out of the room.

"I know your father has a living will," she said when she stopped just outside the door, "and that you're his Power of Attorney. And I understand from the doctor that your father doesn't want to have dialysis, if that would become necessary, or he doesn't want to be hooked up to any machines. What about CPR and any invasive steps that would be necessary?"

"Is he at that point?" Jim asked.

"No. But we need to know his wishes should he go into cardiac arrest."

"What would the invasive steps entail?"

"We would try to revive him with electroshocks to his chest, do a tracheotomy and put a tube in to get his breathing started again. It's not pretty. So we need to know these things now. If anything should happen, we need to know exactly what your father's wishes are so we can act immediately and decisively."

"Can you do the first part without doing the invasive part? I'm not sure he'd want that."

"We could, but it wouldn't do much good. The two go hand in hand. It wouldn't do any good to pound on the chest and get the heart beating, if you don't get the breathing started."

Jim had long been told by his father that he didn't want any dramatic resuscitation when the time came. And he'd made that clear in his living will and his conversations after he'd had open-heart surgery when he was seventy and then reinforced his decision when he had a knee replacement on his good leg when he was seventy-five. He'd gone to an extended-care facility for recovery and therapy for the knee. It was his first time in a nursing home as a patient. He had always gone to visit old friends and family in VA hospitals, civilian hospitals and nursing homes and wished they didn't have to end up in the latter. And after spending some time in the extended-care wing of the nursing home for therapy for three weeks, he was determined that he not end up in the same situation or go to any place of the kind.

At lunch together at the facility just before he was to be released to go home, Jack looked up at his son and said, "Don't you ever put me in one of these sonsabitchin' places."

"What if I have to?"

"You heard what I said. I'll kick the shit out of you."

The memory of that always brought a smile to Jim's face.

"I don't think he would want anything dramatic or invasive done to revive him," Jim said. "That's my understanding. I just want him to be as comfortable as possible for however long he's got yet. That's what he's always told me. And I'm in agreement with him on that."

"Good. I'll tell the doctor. We have a form to get filled out with exactly what CPR procedures we need to follow, get you to sign it and put a wrist band on him that is color coded for what we need to do in case of cardiac arrest."

"I don't recall any of his previous hospital stays that had this sense of urgency about the possibility of death," Jim said. "At least I can't recall any. I thought you said he wasn't at that point. Or maybe it's just that his other surgeries didn't seem to be as life threatening as this trip seems to be shaping up to be. That about it?"

"We just need to have an updated form on file should the need arise, sir."

Truth was that Jack had made all the necessary arrangements in the past and had signed the papers for his Living Will while he was in good health and before he appointed Jim as his Power of Attorney. The old man had always taken care of things and had always pulled through any operation or health problem that came up. "I'm a survivor," he used to tell his son. "You gotta think that way." And Jim wasn't used to the idea or the reality that the time was coming when his father would no longer survive. But it was beginning to sound more and more like this was the time. Or that the time wouldn't be long coming. Maybe that was it. Jim had talked with his father another time about getting him to the VA hospital for any necessary long-term hospital stay.

"You know what I told you about putting me in one of those

sonsabitchin' places," Jack had said. "And I mean it. We're not going to go that route. VA wouldn't be any different."

"What route are we going to take?" Jim had asked.

"We'll cross that bridge when we come to it. Maybe I'll just drop dead."

"Maybe you won't, too. What then?"

"It'll be all right."

Sometime later, neither the old man nor his son could say for sure how long, Jack lay back and said he was still tired but couldn't sleep. It'd been mid-morning when he first got to the emergency room, and the doctors and nurses started poking holes in his arm for IVs, taking blood tests and sticking tabs all over his chest to monitor his heart rate and placing nitroglycerin tablets under his tongue. He seemed to be getting worse rather than better as the day progressed and the early evening winter darkness highlighted the window like a painting of nothingness. Unable to relax or get comfortable, he sat up again, slumped over, kept rubbing his head and wondered when they'd do something to make him feel better or when he'd just die. That'd be okay, too. Get it over with. Make that rendezvous with death sooner rather than later. Die like Betty and Bake and Roc and all the rest. But not to be forgotten. We must not be forgotten. Won't be forgotten.

"I'm ready to die," the old man said in a whisper. "But not to be forgotten."

And he remembered again a passage from Shakespeare's play: "*This day is call'd the Feast of Crispian: He that outlives this day, and comes safe home, Will stand a tip-toe when this day is nam'd and rouse him at the name of Crispian.*" The passage kept rolling through his mind as he lay there thinking about it. That was a long time ago. Who is roused "*at the name of Crispian*" today? Who even knows what it is? Unless they've read Shakespeare? And how many people would that be? Saint Crispian's Day is not even a memory anymore. Would Iwo Jima be the same? The old man once had a bumper sticker on his car that said "Iwo Jima Survivor" and was often stopped in parking lots, gas stations and even once when he was stuck in traffic and thanked for his service. When he'd wear his cap with "Iwo Jima Survivor" on it, the same thing would happen in banks, grocery stores or wherever he went. That always gave him a good feeling. But he'd also begun to run into people who didn't know a thing about Iwo Jima. It was difficult for him to realize that anybody wouldn't know about it. Once when he was getting a haircut in Florida not long after he'd retired from teaching and was spending the winter there, he hung his cap with "Iwo Jima Survivor" printed on it on a coat rack and sat down in the chair.

"What's Iwo Jima?" the young woman had asked as she started clipping his hair.

"What's Iwo Jima?" Jack had parroted the question. "It's an island in the Pacific."

"And you were there?"

"Yes. For a while."

"What were you doing there? Was it during a war?"

"I guess you could say it was during a war. They were shooting at us, anyway."

"Oh, really."

"Really they were. Quite a bit."

"Did you get shot?"

"Yes, I got shot."

"Really? That's too bad. Do you want your sideburns left?"

"Sure. Why not? Make me look spiffy."

"Spiffy?" the woman said and laughed. "Yeah, I'll make you look spiffy."

Jack didn't feel too spiffy then or in the hospital now. He was feeling like the proverbial last rose of summer. That one rose he kept seeing from the wagon back at Aunt Maggie's garden. Just before he was being moved to the intensive care unit earlier in the day, the social service staff member had come by. Jack had heard her talking to somebody about him like he was ready to kick the bucket and go off and join Betty and Bake and Roc and the others who got knocked off back then. It was about time, he thought. He'd had another sixty years after they were gone.

Sixty fucking years that Betty and a whole lot of other good people never had. Can you believe that? How'd that happen? Semper Fi, Mac. Hooray for me and fuck you, huh? I got mine, you get yours. What a shitty deal! Who figured out who died when? And now that you're dying, would they send a preacher man around to hold your hand now that your time has come? To help you get through the ordeal? The inevitable? Father Mallie walked around on the beach, giving last rites to dying Marines and talking to the wounded while the shelling and fighting continued all around them. He was calm and collected, seeming to be oblivious to the war going on around him. He seemed almost invincible, that nothing could touch him.

Not everybody seemed so invincible. The Japs got Bake dead on, Jack knew, just as soon as the incoming mortar round hit and exploded. He could see his best buddy's head ripped off and blood spurting out from the hole where his head had been. Greene and Kelly and Ski were blown to hell and gone, too. Mathews' foot was sitting alone on top of the hole, crookedly pointed south toward Mount Suribachi, some of his guts spilled out in the sand. Childers put a compress over the hole, tied a tourniquet around his leg and hit him with a shot of morphine before moving on to the next wounded Marine. They didn't often see the Jap soldiers. But they were there. And mortars and artillery from both sides and out at sea poured in at any time, hitting somebody when they did. One of them even got the padre before it was all over. A direct hit while he was kneeling over a dying Marine didn't leave enough of either of them to tell who was who.

"What day is it?" Jack heard somebody ask. "Can you tell me what day it is, sweetie?"

"The second Tuesday of next week, sweetie."

"Where are you?"

"In the wagon, sweetie."

"In the wagon?" Jim asked.

"Yeah, dummy," the old man said. "In the fuckin' wagon. Are you blind?"

"I must be blind, Mr. Britton," the blonde ICU nurse said. "I don't see a thing."

"You must be blind as a bat," the old man said. "Can't you see anything, dummy?"

"No, I can't," Jim said. "But you're getting a bit testy there, Dad."

"You'll think testy, you keep treatin' me like this. Who's that woman? She talks funny."

"She's your nurse."

"She talks funny."

"I'm Canadian," the nurse said. "My name's Melanie."

"Melanie, huh? Funny name. You know 'In Flanders Field'?"

"I've heard of it, I think."

"You've heard of it? You've heard of it! It ought to be your goddamn national anthem."

"Relax, Dad, relax."

"I'll relax in the wagon, you nitwit," Jack said. He could see the wagon clearly now and recognized where it sat just behind Aunt Maggie's summer kitchen and in between the vegetable garden and the flower garden. She was walking slowly away from the wagon and toward the blue flowers. The single rose still stood in the ground just out of the old man's reach. He could hear his son talking but didn't hear anything he was saying. Off to the west between Aunt Maggie and the yard fence, the butterflies hovered above the flowers and flitted here and there in search of something they never seemed to find; at least not for long. All day long they fluttered back and forth through the yard and the gardens. They'd dart off somewhere out of sight, and then be back fluttering around again in no time. By nightfall, they found a place they could cling to a limb and rest for the night.

Betty's resting. Bake's off resting, too. And Roc and all the others. Been resting for a long goddamn time. Resting is one way of looking at it, anyway. Betty and he had missed out on a whole life together. Wonder what our life together would have been like, he wondered. All she wanted was to raise a family together, love and be loved. Wonder what kind of a life old Bake would have had had that mortar round not taken him away? Or Roc if the sniper hadn't got him? They were all only seventeen and eighteen and nineteen years old and hadn't talked much about the future. Didn't seem like there was much of one or much to talk about as long as the war was going on, so they didn't talk about it. Oh, Bake had talked once about going to college if he made it home and maybe becoming a teacher. Roc wanted to go to college, too, and work in some kind of business. But that was it. Maybe they would have, too. Maybe they'd have done a lot of things, if they hadn't been killed. Maybe, maybe, maybe. ...

Jack'd been discharged from the hospital and the Marine Corps in early 1946 and, like thousands of other returning GIs from the war, had enrolled in college. He went to the state university on the GI Bill to major in English and become a high school teacher. He'd always liked reading and writing, and after his experiences in the war, he thought he wanted to teach and work with young people, write a little maybe, get married and raise a family. And forget the war. That was the plan. So before he started college, he wanted to marry Betty. He felt as though he'd known her forever and was ready to spend his life with her. She had written to him and kept track of him through a simple code they worked out when he was home on leave before shipping out for Camp Tarawa on the big island in Hawaii to train for the Iwo Jima campaign. When he was going to go into combat, he said he'd write her a letter and ask how her father liked his new car. Which he didn't have, didn't even have a car at the time.

After she received the letter he'd sent from Hawaii before leaving for a landing on some remote, unknown island off in the Pacific that started off, "Hey, Betty, how's your dad like that new car of his by now? I'll bet he's driving the wheels off of it. ..." Betty started looking in the newspapers for the next Marine landing on one of the Pacific Islands. Jack and the rest of the Marines didn't know the name of the island until a couple of days before the landing. They'd only called it Workman

Island in training, if they called it anything. And ninety-nine out of every hundred of them had never heard of Iwo Jima when they were told the name of the island. They were going to secure it in three days and move on toward Japan. When stories started coming in about the bloody campaign the Marines were fighting on Iwo Jima, Betty knew that's where Jack had been headed from Hawaii and that he was there.

To occupy her mind and time and so she could be as aware as she could of what he was going through, Betty clipped anything she found in the area newspapers and put the articles and photos together for a chronological account of what would become one of the most historic battles in the history of warfare. Some twenty thousand Marines of the Fourth and Fifth Marine Divisions landed on the small volcanic island on February 19, 1945, to root out the more than twenty thousand defending Japanese soldiers dug in all over the island and who had pledged to fight until the last man. They were so well defended and fortified that the Third Division, which had originally been kept in reserve, had to be brought in early to help the other two. With supporting troops from all the branches of service, that made a total force of between seventy thousand and eighty thousand Marines, sailors, soldiers and airmen on Iwo Jima before the island was finally secured. With so many of the Marines who fought on Iwo Jima being killed or wounded, it was the bloodiest campaign in Marine Corps history. More than sixty-eight hundred Americans, most of them Marines, were killed in battle for the island and another almost seventeen thousand were wounded, a full third of all Marine casualties in the Marine Corps' forty-three months of service in the Pacific during World War II.

Nearly all of the Japanese soldiers and sailors died in the

fierce thirty-six-day battle for the airstrips on the island needed for crippled USA B-29 bombers to land when they returned from attacks on Japan prior to the planned invasion there. If the crippled planes couldn't make it to the airstrips at Saipan, Tinian or Guam, where the flights originated, they crashed into the sea, taking their crews down with them. Nor could the Japanese on Iwo Jima warn Tokyo of the coming attacks or send out fighter planes to harass the bombers after Iwo Jima fell. And the Iwo Jima story unfolded day by day in Betty's scrapbook. Jack's picture and the accompanying news story about him getting wounded, the telegram that informed his parents he'd been wounded, his letters and then a few pictures of him and Bake and Roc and Dubois and Ski and Robinson and Greene and Kelly and Childers and Wilson and Mathews ... were all there when he was home and out of the service for good. Jack was amazed when he saw the scrapbook and learned details about the battle he hadn't known.

Right near the end of the campaign when the Marines were ready to leave the island and had turned in their live ammunition, a group of some five hundred Japanese soldiers formed at the north end of the island and moved south toward Mount Suribachi in one last desperate *banzai* attack. They overran a group of three hundred airmen sleeping in tents, unguarded and armed only with .45 automatic pistols, and killed one hundred of them before a mostly black Marine Pioneer battalion drove the Japanese away after killing some three hundred of them. That was the last Iwo Jima story in Betty's scrapbook. The last picture in the book was of him and her on their wedding day, walking happily off to their car and into the future together.

With the GI Bill, a part-time job each and the belief that they could have the life they wanted, Jim and Betty got along well and enjoyed college life and being together. He'd never thought he had a chance to go to college when he was growing up. His father had farmed his small home place and worked in the lime quarry to support the family. Jack might have wound up there had it not been for the war. The war gave him some wounds for which he received a small pension and his service in the Marine Corps gave him the GI Bill. He'd rather had his leg and full use of his right hand and arm. But it seemed like a fair exchange to him, under the circumstances, for the price he'd paid and what he'd lost forever. Taken all together, he was able to go to college and Betty and he were able to get married. When he learned that was going to be possible, he went and bought Betty an engagement ring and a small heart necklace filled with gold shavings. He was going to ask her to marry him right away and took them with him to dinner on her birthday. After they'd had a drink, talked awhile and ordered dinner, he'd pulled the necklace out of his pocket and placed it beside her plate when she'd turned her head.

"What's this?" she asked when she looked back and saw the necklace.

"It's a heart of gold," he said, holding out the ring. "Mine, that I'd like you to have if you'll marry me and spend your life with me. And here's a ring, too, if you'll say yes."

"Oh, Jack, I've always hoped for this," she said, tears streaming down her cheeks as she accepted his proposal. "Of course, I'll marry you, you silly man. I love you so much."

He didn't think he'd ever been any happier in his life. They had a small wedding in Betty's church in the country and went to the university to start their new life together as their honeymoon. Both of them always said setting up housekeeping, starting their marriage and pursuing their dreams was the greatest honeymoon anybody could have. The university felt like the place they should be. Jack had picked it like he used to pick foxholes: It just felt right.

"You're a lucky man, Britt," Bowman said after the wedding. "And you deserve it."

"So do you, buddy," Jack said. "Don't you ever forget that."

Jack knew he was lucky. He wasn't having as hard a time as Bowman, had a great wife and had accepted what had happened in the war and only had occasional nightmares about getting caught behind enemy lines and being tortured by the Japs; his wounds were bearable, and he was thankful for what he had with Betty and went off to college for two years before Jim was born. Those two years together were the happiest of Jack's life. And the couple was quite happy when they learned Betty was pregnant. She had an easy pregnancy, feeling good all through it. Then when her due date came and went, she started swelling up more than the doctor thought normal when he examined her. He scheduled her to come in at eight o'clock the next morning and would induce labor, if she hadn't delivered normally. Jack and some of his friends stood watch just outside the bedroom that night and played fifty-cent-limit poker until seven a.m. Saturday morning. At seven, everybody tossed in his cards and wished him good luck as they all left the house. Betty was awake when he got to the bedroom, sitting up with a pillow at her back.

"Good morning," he said, bending down and kissing her lips. "Been awake long?"

"Whew," she said. "You reek of coffee and cigarettes. But no, I just woke up when I heard the guys leaving. That was nice of them to sit up with you."

"Yeah, and they left me a few bucks to buy breakfast with," Jack said and laughed. "That was real nice of them, too. You feeling okay? Ready to do this?"

"I'm ready to get it over with. It's been miserable the past few days, but I don't feel too bad this morning. A little nervous, maybe."

But when she went into the hospital for the delivery, the problems began. Her contractions started coming early in the morning and continued throughout the day and on into the night. They were not close together and caused more pain and anxiety than anything else. Jack had gone to the hospital cafeteria and got breakfast after they got Betty checked in and in a room. Then he came back and stayed with her until the baby was ready to come. At a little before noon the next day, they wheeled her toward the delivery room. Her labor pains were coming every three minutes now, and the doctor said the baby would be born any time.

"Please hurry," Betty said, "Please. It hurts so much."

"I love you, Betty," Jack said, bending down to kiss her before she was taken into the delivery room where he was not allowed. It was okay to send him into hell on a godforsaken island where human flesh was violently ripped off of bodies or burned or hideously maimed, but he was not permitted to witness the birth of new life — his own child. What bullshit, he'd thought. And the doctor made him feel both angry and sad when he'd told Jack that the last thing he "needed in a delivery room was a nervous husband who would only be in the way."

"The last thing I need to hear is that kind of bullshit," Jack said. "I know enough to stay out of the way."

The doctor didn't answer.

Betty squeezed Jack's hand and cried out in pain. "Oh, it hurts," she said.

"There, there, honey," the anesthetist said. "It doesn't hurt that much."

"A helluva lot you know about it. You never had a baby."

Jack laughed then and patted her hand. She was doing just fine. Then he watched the doctor, the anesthetist and four nurses surrounding Betty from a six-by-six-inch window in the door to the delivery room. He couldn't see anything except the backs of the nurses on one side of Betty. He didn't know about the toxemia then. It hadn't been discovered until the last minute, and he wasn't told about it. By then, it was too late to do anything, even if there'd been anything that could have been done.

A few minutes after noon, Betty delivered a nine-pound, eleven-ounce healthy boy they'd already agreed to name James Albert after Bake and Roc. Jack saw the doctor lift the baby and give him to a waiting nurse who took him to clean him up and cut the umbilical cord, then turn back to Betty and begin to work frantically. A nurse brought the baby to the window and held him up for Jack to see. A burst of pride surged through his body as he realized that his son had just been born a few feet away and now rested just on the other side of the door. But he was concerned about Betty. The doctor and the nurses continued to huddle around her and seemed to still be working frantically away for some reason.

Twenty minutes later, the doctor walked to the door to

bring Jack the bad news: Betty had died on the delivery table. Her blood pressure had skyrocketed to 260/130, and she had gone into cardiac arrest. Efforts to revive her were unsuccessful and she had died.

"I'm sorry, Mr. Britton, but your wife didn't make it."

"Didn't make it? What the hell do you mean, she 'didn't make it,' Doc? You mean she's dead? She's dead?"

"I'm afraid so. Apparently she had developed toxemia, something that comes on at the last minute, and we have no effective treatment for at this time. It strikes about one in ten thousand women at childbirth and is often fatal. The blood pressure shoots up dangerously high, and the body effectively shuts down just after delivery in most cases. That's what happened to your wife. There's nothing we could do. I'm very sorry, Mr. Britton."

"Yeah, me too," Jack said, tightening his facial muscles and squinting his eyes to suppress the feelings of anger he was having.

How is this possible? I've come to terms with the possibility of my own death on Iwo but not Betty's here like this. Not lovely Betty with the honey brown hair and the blue-green eyes and perky little nose and lithe athletic body. Not the beautiful woman who took me less than whole and gave me hope for life. Losing her is a fate worse than death. What the fuck? Why God? Why'd you let me live to come back to this shit? Why didn't you just let me die on that stinking fucking little island, if this is what you had in store for me? Why didn't you leave me there with Bake and Roc? None of us would ever have to face this shit then. "I'm sorry as hell, too, Doc. Just about as fuckin' sorry as I can fuckin' be."

"I know how you feel."

"You do, huh? I doubt that very much. But what about the baby?"

"Baby's fine. A healthy boy."

"I just don't understand," Jack said. He remembered when the replacement lieutenant had been hit by a mortar round and blew both legs off one morning up by Hill 362A just before he'd been hit himself. Hell, they'd kept the lieutenant alive for the rest of the day. He died but he hadn't died immediately. And Betty was just having a baby, not taking a direct hit. How could she die having a baby? Women had babies every day.

"It's just the luck of the draw," the doctor said. "Happens rarely, but when it does —"

"When it does, it fucks up the family it happens to," Jack said and spun on his heel and walked away. He felt alone, the same kind of aloneness he'd felt when Bake and Roc and Larson and Robinson and Ski and all the others had got hit or died along the way. He was left to continue alone, much like he'd been left in the war. Only then after he'd been hit, he'd been thrown in with others who were also wounded, many much more seriously than he had been, but they shared a common bond. It was different now. He didn't know anyone else who had just lost a wife and had a new baby to raise. After he had been hit and as soon as he was able and found where others from the company were hospitalized, he went to visit them. Most were happy to see him, to know that he'd made it. But he was visibly shaken when he went to visit Oliver, a man he hadn't been particularly close to but had known since boot camp in '43. Oliver had been paralyzed from the waist down after shrapnel from a mortar round severed his spinal cord.

"Hey, Bull," Jack said when he saw him. "How you doin'?"

"Get the hell out of here and don't ever come back," Oliver said, yelling at the top of his voice just as soon as he saw Jack and in a manner that was totally out of character. He had always been a big, strong, nice guy, a friend to all before that. "I don't ever want to see any of you fuckin' guys again. Now get the hell out of here and leave me the fuck alone. Forever."

At the time, Jack had just thought the hell with him and left the ward. As time passed, he came to a much better appreciation of what it must have been like for Oliver at that very young age to be permanently paralyzed from the waist down for the rest of his life. Then Jack thought he knew better the reaction Oliver had had and why. He'd always been a man's man, able to do anything physically and keep up with anyone. That was no longer possible. He'd still be able to have a relationship of sorts with women, but it would never be the same for him as it was for the others or as it had been before, either. Someone in the hospital had told Jack something he wasn't sure could happen. When the nurse was bathing him that Oliver supposedly started getting an erection. The nurse had told him to get those thoughts out of his mind, that he wasn't going to be able to do anything about it, now or ever. But nothing worked. She even told him to think of vomit and everything else rotten, to no avail. Finally, the nurse reportedly took a ruler and whacked his penis with a quick, hard snap, and he lost the erection. Jack had always wondered how Oliver had gotten along through the years and always wondered if he was another suicide victim of Iwo. Getting left behind wasn't easy. That's what always bothered him. It wasn't the dying that seemed so hard, it was the living and carrying on after everybody else died and you got left behind with all the baggage.

And now he had been left behind again.

Somehow, Jack took care of all the arrangements for Betty's funeral with their parents by his side, got through the funeral and took young James Albert to his parent's home to stay for a while. During the next few days, he set things up for the baby in his little house and at both grand-parents who'd agreed to help him raise the boy. Then he took off for the next two weeks and headed out to Bake's family in western Pennsylvania.

He'd written to his parents while he was in the Great Lakes hospital and had promised to visit someday. That hadn't worked out before. But now he didn't know any place he'd rather be than with his best buddy's family. The night he arrived in the small Pennsylvania town across the state line from Ohio, the whole family gathered at Bake's folks house and had supper and several drinks and exchanged stories about their son, their brother and their friend. It was a happier time for them after so much sadness. It was a much-needed diversion for Jack. One of his favorite stories happened at Camp Pendleton before their outfit shipped out to Camp Tarawa in Hawaii to train for the Iwo Jima landing.

"A couple of guys in another platoon took a dislike to us for some reason," Jack said. "I never did know what it was over but probably some imagined slight, or even a real one. I don't know what it was. But how could anyone dislike us since we were both such sweet, fellow Marines? We thought we were quite likable."

"Come on now," Bake's older brother Johnny said. He had also survived Iwo Jima and had fought on Guam with the Marines but had joined the Army and was home on leave before heading back to Europe. "I met you guys on Iwo and know a little about Gyrines myself. You guys had to do something. I knew Jim pretty well. He could get under your skin in a minute. I used to chase him all over this place when we were kids."

Jack laughed along with the family before continuing.

"No, really," he said, "I can't think of a thing that got them started. I don't even remember their names, but one was a big redhead from down South. Anyway, they began doing everything they could to antagonize us. Jim usually led the retaliation. Nothing real bad or violent. He was more of a prankster. Silly stuff like short-sheeting their racks. So when they got in, the sheet had been doubled so they could only get halfway in bed. One thing I remember clearly occurred when we were billeted in a Quonset hut somewhere that had an air vent on top. Bake — Jim — had the top bunk and these guys found it out, so one of them waited until we were in the sack, climbed up on the roof, pulled the protector off of the vent and poured a bucket of cold water down on top of Bake, dousing him and his bunk. He was fit to be tied."

Johnny howled with laughter; the rest of the family joined in.

"I'll bet he was," he said. "What did Big Jim do?"

"He was so mad he jumped up and chased the guy all over the area but couldn't catch him. Woke the whole company and had everybody P.O.'d."

"I wouldn't have wanted to be him if Jim had caught him."

"Neither would I. He could be a bear."

"Yeah," Bill, another brother said. "I remember one time we'd been out camping and everybody got soaked. We undressed and hung our clothes up to dry while we pranced around the fire as naked as a jaybird. I dressed before my clothes were quite dry and knocked Jim's in the dirt. I picked his shirt up and held it up for him to see it. I tossed it back in the dirt and picked up his trousers, showed him the dirt and tossed them back to the ground. When Jim saw me tossing his clothes back on the ground and laughing, he lowered his head, lunged at me and missed. I kicked his clothes and took off running. Never caught me. It was a sight seeing him naked and chasing me all around the campsite. Even though I was a couple of years older, I didn't want to get into it with him while he was so mad. Wouldn't have been pretty."

"Well, it was like that with these guys all the time we were at Pendleton and Camp Tarawa," Jack said. "But here's the strange thing: On Iwo they both came up to us and apologized, said they had been out of line, shook hands with us and said that from now on they would be our buddies as Marines should be, that we should fight and die together. We accepted their apology and everything was fine between us from then on. The threat of death does strange things to some people. We welcomed their acceptance of us finally as Marine buddies who would stand together against the real enemy. Which we did. But it was crazy before that."

That sobered things up a bit after the fun and laughter Jack had had with the family. Never once had he mentioned his own problems or acted as though anything was wrong in his life. When he left the next day, everybody followed him out to his car, hugged him and told him to be sure to stay in touch and to come back any time. The next time he came back was for his buddy's memorial service a year later. By that time, Jim's brother Johnny had been killed, too.

The family had had Bake's remains sent home in 1949, as soon as they could, and had buried him in the Bakken family plot.

Jack went to the cemetery after the memorial service for the burial with full military rites. Then he went back with Bake's father, Joe, and visited the cemetery again before he left for home. The simple marker was up and read,

"James L. Bakken PFC USMC

October 2, 1926 — March 2, 1945

Iwo Jima

World War II"

"It's hard to believe," Jack said. "Seems like he should be standing here, too."

"His mother hasn't recovered yet," Joe said, "from losing two of her three boys. Jim was our second son and died first. That hit her real hard. As you know, Johnny served in the Marines, too. He survived the rest of the war but came home and fell in love with a great young woman whose parents were real religious. Her father was a preacher. And they didn't think Johnny was good enough for her. He was kind of rowdy after coming home from the war. He wanted to work in construction and own his own company someday. They wanted a proper young man, somebody who didn't drink and fight like Johnny did after he got home. He was pretty wild for quite a while. So when Johnny and her got serious, and he was starting to settle down, her parents sent her off for the summer and said they'd never have a thing to do with her, if she ended up with him. Real hard for the girl to go against her folks when they put it like that, I guess. Broke Johnny's heart, though. He stayed drunk most of the time for the next three weeks, ran out of money and joined the Army. Said that was where he belonged, anyway. He went to Europe to help rebuild it after the war; stationed in Trieste, Italy. Worked in a construction battalion, learning what he wanted to do. Figured he'd start his own company when he retired from the Army and was doing okay. Sounded good in his letters. I was happy for him. Went out with another soldier one night on the guy's motorcycle last spring. He missed a curve, went off the road and hit a tree. Broke Johnny's neck. The other guy only got a broken leg.

"We were both depressed. I was mad and hurt like hell. But it almost killed her. Now we'd lost two sons in the service. Alice hardly ever got a good night's sleep after Jim got killed. Then we went through it again when Johnny got killed. His body got here in April, just before we learned that Jim would be sent home in July. She hardly slept until the caskets got here. Only then could she sleep, but it took awhile for that to happen. And she still only catnaps."

It had taken Jack a long time before he could sleep, too, after he returned from Iwo Jima and had been released from the hospital and was out on his own. Just about the time he was getting to the point where he could sleep part of the night and only have a nightmare now and then, Betty died and left him with a baby son. What they'd hoped for. He loved the little boy, loved to hold him in his arms and watch him take in the new world around him. But there was a part of him that resented the baby boy that had lived while his mother had died. He knew that was not thinking straight. Yet the thought was always there. Why did Betty die and the boy live? How come Bake and so many others didn't make it? Just because that's the way it is? Couldn't be any other way. Betty was the love of his life, the most beautiful woman he'd ever seen. She could brighten up his world wherever they were. He'd thought of her while he was on Iwo Jima and thought of their life together when he had a minute to do so. He knew she'd be there for him just like he knew Bake would be right there for him.

And Roc and the others, too. They were all the kind of people you could depend on. You could trust them to watch your back., Cover your ass. Come to the rescue. Or just do whatever needed to be done, when it needed to be done. Like the time he and Bake were on liberty in San Diego, walking down the street, headed for a bar to find what they considered "a little action" and Bake helped avoid a fight. A sailor and a very drunk but pretty woman came staggering toward them. The sailor wasn't staggering as much as he was helping the woman along. When the woman saw Jack and Bake, she immediately left the sailor and came toward them.

"A Marine, a Marine," she said and threw her arms around Jack. "I love Marines."

The sailor grabbed her and said, "I saw her first, Mac."

"That's fine with me," Jack said. "You can have her."

"Why, you Jarhead sonuvabitch," the woman said and slugged him in the stomach. "I'm not good enough for you, huh?"

The sailor lunged toward him and tried to hit Jack over the back of the woman. Bake stepped between the woman and the sailor and held up his hand.

"Back off, swab," he said. "Ain't nothing to this."

Jack grabbed the woman's hand as she tried again to swing and said, "You can have her, Mac. Semper Fi. I've got mine. She's all yours."

Now both Bake and Betty and all the others were gone. Vanished into thin air, leaving big empty holes in Jack Britton's life. Going on was hard. He'd left the Bakkens the first time and headed aimlessly out across the country, never knowing where he was going and stopping only when he was tired, sleepy or needed gas. Sometimes he slept in the car; sometimes he took a bedroll and slept out on the ground nearby. He remembered seeing the presidents' faces they'd been carving into Mt. Rushmore for years and the Golden Gate Bridge spanning San Francisco Bay. But he didn't remember much in between. Only that he'd driven straight through the day and night the first couple of days and then wound around aimlessly, turning whatever direction he felt like. Somewhere in the mountains west of Denver, he'd picked up a hitchhiker and took him about a hundred miles before stopping abruptly in a small town and telling him to get out.

"What's wrong?" the hitchhiker asked. "I thought you were going to San Francisco."

"I don't know where the fuck I'm going," Jack said. "But I need to be alone. So get out."

He did end up in San Francisco and headed south along the coast. More than one night, he pulled the car off on the beach or on some pullout from the road and slept for an hour or two. His money was running low by the time he got close to Los Angeles. Early one evening, he pulled up in front of the Hollywood USO where Bake, Roc and a whole group of them had stopped one evening on liberty before leaving the States for Hawaii. That was not quite five years before, but it seemed like a lifetime. Jack took a cup of coffee and slumped over the counter. It was Friday evening, and servicemen started drifting in, looking lost and not knowing quite what to do with their free time. They looked so young to Jack. He was only twenty-three but felt much older. About nine o'clock, he heard two Marines talking about going home on leave to Texas.

"We can get home faster hitchhiking that we can on that damn bus," one of them said. "Took me four days to get to Waco when I went home last Christmas. We had a breakdown out in the desert not far out of Needles and liked to never get out of there. Would've taken almost three days, if we hadn't broke down."

"But we got to get out somewhere where we can hitchhike," the other one said. "We can't just go out here on Hollywood Boulevard and stick out our thumbs. We'd have every fag out dragging the boulevard stopping and trying to suck our dicks. Never would get to Texas."

"I'm heading back that way," Jack said. "And I ain't no fag. Used to wear that uniform."

The two Marines laughed and turned to look at him. He wasn't particularly going to Texas, but he was ready for some company and could get a few bucks from them for gas and food to get home. He felt as though he were going home on leave again, too.

"Let's find a couple more people headed east and get on the road," he said. "Give me fifty bucks apiece and you'll be in Texas before you know it. I'll take you right to your door."

"That's pretty steep, buddy. I'm from right close to Abilene."

Jack shrugged. "I'm busted, a long the way from home. I've got a car, a '42 Ford that runs like a sewing machine. You guys got some bucks and want to get home, fast. So do I."

"There's a couple of sailors over there from the Panhandle," the first Marine said. "Let's get 'em, and we'll all give you forty a piece. How 'bout that? I'm ready to roll."

"That'll work. I'm ready, too."

Twenty minutes later, Jack, the two Marines and two sailors walked to the car and stowed four seabags in the trunk of the two-door coupe, crammed into the car and headed toward Pasadena where they could get on Route 66 and head east. The sun was still high in the sky behind them as Jack turned out on the highway and saw that everybody was getting comfortable.

"Before you guys crash out," he said, "I think I can handle it most of the night. May have to have a cup of coffee now and then. We can get a sandwich or something when I stop for gas. Other than that, let's keep it on the road. I'll need some help driving then."

Jack felt a sense of relief, a sense of everything being okay, to be heading east and heading home. He fairly flew through the night and through Barstow and Needles and on through Arizona. By Sunday morning, he had turned the driving over to Brummet, one of the Marines, and was dozing in the passenger's seat when the car topped a hill just west of Gallup, New Mexico, and ran into a speed trap. Brummet had hollered out, waking everybody, and hit the brakes hard as he was rolling down the hill at seventy-five miles an hour or more. One officer stood at the side of the road waving cars to pull over and stop.

"Goddamn, I don't have any driver's license," Brummet said. "What am I going to do?"

"Use mine," the other Marine said, handing his billfold to the front seat. "I'm prettier than you, but we're close enough. We're in uniform. Maybe they'll let us go."

"I wouldn't count on that," Jack said, looking out at the line of cars ahead of them and several uniformed officers writing tickets as fast as they could. "Looks like a Sunday morning go-to-court speed trap where everybody pays the piper."

A heavy-set deputy stepped up to the car and looked in after Brummet had rolled down the window, raised his hand and counted the five young men in the car. "Looks like you boys are in a hurry," he said. "Where you headed in such a hurry?"

"Home to Texas," Brummet said. "Abilene. My mother's in the hospital there, and my cousin and me have emergency leave to go home to see her."

"Sorry to hear that. This your car?"

"No sir," Brummet said, pointing over to Jack. "The car is his. We caught a ride with him in LA. The sailors, too."

"Well, we clocked you at eighty-two miles an hour comin' over that hill. I'm goin' have to give you a ticket, son. You can stop by the courthouse and pay the ticket as you go through town."

"It's Sunday morning," Brummet said. "Courthouse open?"

"Yes, sir, it is," the deputy said, handing him the license and the ticket. "Courthouse is two blocks to the right as you go through town. You'll see where it is right away. Hope your mom gets along okay."

"Can you believe this shit?" Brummet asked no one in particular. "It's Sunday morning and these assholes have a speed trap out and the courthouse is open. Look at that fuckin' line."

From there on into town, a steady line of cars pulled off the shoulder in front of them and behind them and drove directly to the courthouse. The area around it and throughout the downtown area was packed with cars with out-of-state license plates. People filled the street, and a line spilled out the courthouse door and onto the sidewalk.

Brummet drove slowly by and found a place right in front as a car pulled out.

"Here's fifty bucks for the fine," Jack said, handing him the money. "Won't be that much. But take your buddy with you and tell them that story about getting the emergency leave and see if you can get to the head of the line. Otherwise, we'll be here all day."

The sailors were already asleep when Jack laid his head back and dozed off. He'd watched the Marines in dress greens walk up to the line and then talk to someone at the door. A few minutes later, they walked back out and headed for the car.

"I hope my momma ain't sick and in the hospital," Brummet said when he got to the car. "But like you said, Jack, we would've been here all day, otherwise. There must have been a hundred people in that courtroom. It was unbelievable."

"Probably more than that," the other Marine said. "You see the glares we got when the bailiff took us up to see the judge? They were pissed off being there in the first place and more pissed off seeing us go to the head of the line."

"That's life," Jack said. "They'll get over it."

"Here's fifteen bucks, Jack," Brummet said. "Thanks. I'll watch the speed."

"I can drive for a while now," Jack said. "Just pull up to a gas station and we'll get some gas and some sandwiches somewhere and get on the road."

Back on the highway again, they soon found a gas station with a restaurant nearby. While the attendant was filling the tank and checking the oil, Jack went to the restaurant and ordered a dozen hamburgers and a half dozen bottles of sarsaparilla. He was really feeling good, heading east. The sun wasn't quite overhead yet, and he wondered where he'd be when the sun disappeared over the western horizon. Closer to home, wherever it was, he knew.

"It ain't the greatest breakfast in the world, boys," Jack said. "But there's two or three hamburgers and a sarsaparilla for each of us. We've got '*miles to go before we sleep.*'"

For the rest of the day and into the night, Jack pushed the

old car east and then southeast toward Lubbock and Abilene. He stopped only for gas or to use a toilet and not long then. He was still driving along in the early morning when one of the sailors popped up and said, "Next town is Littlefield. That's where I live. You can just drop me off at the stop sign."

"I'll take you to your house."

For the next hundred miles, he pulled off the road twice and dropped the other sailor at his home in Snyder, then the Marine at his house in Sweetwater and headed on east. Brummet was the last one to go. He got out of the car in Trent, a small town outside of Abilene, and Jack waved and drove away. He bought a case of beer in Abilene and headed north by northeast through the country, nursing the beer along until the sun had gone down and come up again. About seven o'clock in the morning he saw a little truck stop he recognized and pulled in for breakfast. With a plate of biscuits and gravy and four mugs of strong, hot coffee, Jack was ready to head home, see his son and get back to school. It was time. He wondered how the rest of his life would be. Whatever came, he was ready for it.

For the next hour or so, the hospital room was quiet except for the television tuned to CNN. It was reported that more American Marines and soldiers had been killed in ambushes and roadside bombings in Iraq. The Humvee the Marines were in was sitting halfway off the road, half-burned and useless. Two Marines stood off to the side while an officer talked to the CNN reporter and told him what had happened only minutes earlier. A pair of boots stuck out from the backside of the Humvee from one of the dead Marines. One of the wounded sat on the ground with his head in his hands. The old man swore and saw the beach was full of wounded Marines now, lying in makeshift tents and on the sand. Night passed slowly. He heard an occasional scream or somebody hollering for a corpsman. Otherwise, it was quiet, almost peaceful. He lay back in the wagon and closed his eyes. His son dozed fitfully in a chair nearby while the night crawled along and a dark pall gathered throughout the room. Every now and then, the nurse or someone else would come to the edge of the curtain, look in at the monitors and see the old man asleep and step back. Jack came awake for the ten o'clock news and saw that the Bulls had won the game against the Pistons and were continuing their comeback after a dismal start.

"Hear that, you old fart?" Jim asked. "Looks like the Bulls are going to make the playoffs. You told me they were done before the season even started."

"I heard," Jack said, barely whispering. "Don't count your chickens yet. This is a Chicago team we're talking about. The Cubs lost a playoff spot last fall when they choked, like they always do; the Bears haven't had a decent team in so long I've forgotten what it's like for them to win anything; and the Bulls will probably lose before it's all over. I lose all the way around with my teams. But I'm still here and still rooting for the losers. Wonder what that says about me? Rooting for the wrong teams, knowing I'm not going to have any winners."

Bake didn't make it, but he was a winner, Jack thought. He just happened to be in the wrong place at the wrong time. If I'd have been six inches the other way, I'd have had my head blown off; six inches the other way, and I'm untouched. How the hell you figure anything like that? Coming in, boats with thirty young men, boys really, seventeen and eighteen and nineteen years old, had been blown out of the water. Kids dying before they reached the shores of Iwo Jima. Dying just as soon as they hit the beach. Dying before they lived. Dying, dying, dying, Marines still dying on the beach, forever dying. Dying in the desert in Iraq in a different kind of war and in a different time. But still dying, dying, dying. ...

"I'm dying," the old man whispered hoarsely. "And I want all these fuckin' old tubes out of me, and I want to go home and die peacefully."

"I asked the nurse to take the tube out of your stomach. She's calling the doctor. There was some bleeding, I guess, is the reason they put the tube in—"

"I told that idiotic doctor I couldn't take aspirin a month ago," the old man said, his eyes flashing anger. "Kept insisting I take it. Makes my old guts bleed. They don't know shit around here. Dumbest bunch of fuckin' people I've ever been around in my life."

"—and they want that line in your artery to get an accurate blood pressure reading—"

"They can stay out of my business. That's none of their business. Nosiest fuckin' people I've ever seen. And they don't know a thing. Dumber 'n owl shit."

"—It's been pretty high."

"I'm sure of that," Jack said and dozed off. He could see Betty floating above him, smiling and beckoning him to her. Her long light brown hair fell to her shoulders and moved up and down as she floated around above him. He tried to reach out for her, but she moved higher up and just out of reach. She was so beautiful that he was satisfied just watching her. It was like the first time he'd seen her after he got to Great Lakes. His wounds were healing, and he was adjusting to how it was going to be for the rest of his life. Some days he felt as though he could do just about anything; other days he wasn't sure how he was going to be able to live with a crippled-up hand and arm and no foot. He was conscious of how his hand looked and struggled to learn to use it to do what he'd always done with it. He was beginning to use his left hand for everything and was proud of that. He'd always been ambidextrous. It wasn't any big deal on the wards with men with all kinds of wounds and injuries. Going back home was going to be different. But Betty took care of any problems he could have had the first time she came to visit.

They held each other for several minutes before they said anything. It'd been more than two years since he'd seen her and held her. He stepped back and looked at her eyes.

"You're so beautiful, Betty," he said. "What'd I ever do to deserve you?"

"I'm so glad you made it back, Jack," she said, crying softly. "I love you so much and when I started following the landing on Iwo Jima and saw how awful it was and how many Marines were dying, I wasn't sure I'd ever see you again. But you made it."

"Yes, I made it. I don't know how, but I made it. I love you, god, I love you, Betty."

Later, they sat at a table and talked. They'd kept up with each other by letter, and Betty knew about the degree of Jack's wounds. She took his pink and shriveled right hand in hers and lifted it to her lips. Her eyes glistened as she kissed the hand.

"I'm so sorry for you, Jack, for all you've been through."

"I'm one of the lucky ones, Betty. Lucky to be here, lucky to have you."

After he got home and got to be alone with her, she'd undressed him and had him lie back on the bed while she ran her hands over his entire body. She caressed his hand first, then ran both hands lightly up his arm and over the hole in his shoulder. He lay quietly, looking at her as she removed his prosthesis and placed it on the floor. Neither of them had said a word, but both had tears rolling down their cheeks by the time she had looked carefully at the stump of his leg. Then she undressed and lay down beside him and let him hold her in his arms. They lay there for the longest time, not saying a word and drifted off to sleep. Jack thought that he could have lain there forever, not making love or even talking, she had made him feel so good.

And then he'd lost her and had to go on without her, too. But like the others, she'd left him with something that helped him go on. He'd never figured out how or why some people came back from the war and seemed to get along and others just couldn't find the handle. Different people internalized the same things in entirely different ways. Of course. But how could some end up killing themselves like Arnold and Bowman and some of the others while so many went on with life and did well? The old man stirred restlessly, memories of long ago and questions with no answers flashing through his mind. He was disturbed.

A little before midnight, he sat up and started to swing his legs off the bed.

"Whoa, whoa, Dad," Jim said, jumping out of the chair where he'd been sleeping. "You can't get out of bed."

"The hell I can't. I've got to use the bathroom."

"You're all hooked up. They've got a catheter in you, and you've been using the bedpan. I'll call the nurse."

"What nurse? I've got to shit; I don't need a goddamn nurse to shit."

Jim hit the call button and pushed his father's legs back in bed. The nurse saw what was happening as she walked around the pulled curtain and said something the old man couldn't make out. But he recognized what he thought was a patronizing tone.

"I don't know what you said, don't know who you are or what you're doin' here. But I don't need a thing from you. Not a goddamn thing. Get out of here. I've got to shit, and I'm going to go do it, if I can get this idiot here out of the way. This idiot's trying to keep me from shitting, too. What's the matter with you people?"

"Let me get the bedpan for you, Mr. Britton."

"You're an idiot, too. Just plain stupid. I'm getting out of this wagon, and I'm getting out of this here place. Beats anything I ever saw. You tend to your own business."

The old man kept up the same hostile, aggressive, insulting talking for the next hour or so. It wore on Jim, but he'd never seen his father like that before and knew it was totally out of character. Sometime during the hour, Jim had asked the nurse for a sedative, but the doctor on call had said no to the sedative just as he had said no to removing the tube from the nose that went down through the throat and into the stomach. When Jim told his father the tube had to stay, the old man opened his eyes and stared angrily at his son and raised his hand to his nose.

"That's a bunch of crap," he said quietly, rubbing the plastic covering that secured the tube to his stomach and covered the oxygen line to his nostrils. "My nose hurts with this stuff in there. Tickles. I can't breath; my throat's dry."

"I'll get you some ice chips," the nurse said and left the room.

"I don't want her to get me a thing," the old man said. "You either."

"You know who I am?" Jim asked.

"Yes, I know who you are. You want to be my boss. You want to boss me around."

The duty nurse brought the ice chips and tried to give the old man a small spoonful.

He turned his head and said rather loudly, "Get her out of here. Who is she anyway?"

"I'm the nurse on duty to take care of you tonight," the young woman said. "Who are you, sir? My name's Melanie. I'll be here for you all night. Just let me know what you need."

"You sound funny, talk funny."

"I'm French-Canadian," the nurse said, again trying to give the old man some ice chips. "Remember me telling you that earlier?"

"Get that away from me," the old man said, pushing the spoon away from him with the back of his hand. "Where do you find these idiots? They're all just a bunch of idiots. I got to shit, I tell you. Now get out of my way."

"Why don't you take a break, Dad, and let them get the bedpan?" Jim asked as he took the glass of ice chips from the nurse and shrugged while he pushed his father's feet back in bed. "How 'bout some ice for that dry throat?"

The old man's eyes softened as he opened his mouth and took a spoonful of ice chips like a baby bird taking a worm from its father's or mother's beak. Jim continued talking softly and tried to reason with his father. At this point, he just seemed to be angry and a bit confused. He'd slowed down in the last few years, but his mind was still sharp. And he never acted like he had been acting. He was normally polite and courteous to people. Jim had heard about all his father had been through in the war and then survived to come home and lose his wife and keep on surviving. The more the old man talked, and the more he saw his father's response, the more it was apparent that there was something else going on that his father couldn't control, something besides the war and all the people in his life who hadn't survived. When Jack dozed, Jim finally got a chance to go out to the nurse's desk and asked about the angry reactions and delusional comments.

"What's with all the hostility and aggressiveness?" he asked. "Dad's not like that."

"It's pretty common here in the ICU," Melanie said.

"Yeah, somebody's always pulling out lines or doing something bizarre during the night," a heavy-set, middle-aged male nurse named Miles said. "Happens all the time. At night. Throughout the night. Most every night. Had a man over here a couple of nights ago tear out his central line."

"Hurt him?"

"Not really. Didn't seem to, anyway. He sent flowers a couple of days later."

"So they remember what they do?"

"Sometimes they remember parts of it," Melanie said. "Sometimes they don't remember anything. Just according to who it is, I guess, or how bad it gets."

"And it just happens at night?"

"That's right. Seems like it's all over when the sun comes up, too. Most of the time. They just get in here, get confused with the reaction to the medication, the surroundings or the chemical balance in their bodies. Something. Whatever it is, they sort of go nuts at night and are over it by morning. Just goes away when the sun comes streaming through those windows."

"That's strange. I don't think I've ever heard of anything like that."

"You're not around an ICU every night," Miles said, smiling. "It's worse during a full moon when all the werewolves are out, I think. But it's something else. The phenomenon is called sundown syndrome, midnight or sleep-deprivation psychosis, ICU psychosis or whatever else you might hear. They're called sundowners. Any number of things might cause it. Who knows? You've just got to ride it out and wait for morning. Get a job in a hospital and you'll see it all the time."

"No thanks," Jim said. "I'll pass on that. Sounds like they're all 'raging against the dying of the light.' The old man, my father, sure has been raging through the night tonight — 'raging against the dying of the light,' too. He's been impossible. That's completely out of character for him. I never saw anything like it. He's usually a nice guy. Oh, he can be blunt and straightforward, but he's never obnoxious and doesn't talk to people like he's been talking to us tonight. You folks do a great job, but I wouldn't want it. If this sundown thing has anything to do with his behavior, I'm sure ready for the night to pass for him to start acting more normal again."

Back at the side of the bed, it wasn't clear whether the old man would ever be normal again. Maybe it was the onset of Alzheimer's or some arcane disease that robbed old people of their minds before the rest of the body gave out and shut down. The old man had had much wrong with him through the years. But he was remarkably strong and resilient. He always bounced back and kept coming. Open-heart surgery, infected gall bladder, knee replacement, high blood pressure, weak kidneys and congestive heart failure. He had never let his wounds bother him. And as health problems developed, he handled each the same way. It was something that happened, something he had to deal with as best he could. This time was no different.

"You still here?" the old man asked, looking up in the semi-darkness of the room. The light filtered in from the inner circle of the intensive care unit and gave off a hazy shape to everything in the room. "You might as well go back to your place. And I'm not staying here around these idiots. Who are they anyway? Where'd they come from?"

"They're nurses, Dad. You're in the hospital. In the ICU."

"You're crazy, too. An idiot just like all the rest. This is not a hospital. I've been in a bunch of hospitals. I don't know what you call this fuckin' place, but it sure as hell is not a hospital. I feel like hell, and I've gotten worse since all you idiots have been around me. I'm dying is what I'm doing. Let's go ahead and get it over with."

Jim looked up at the monitor and saw the heart rate and blood pressure jump to more than a hundred for the pulse and to 240/115 for the blood pressure. The danger lights were flashing as the numbers stood out on the monitor. Stroke numbers, cardiac arrest. No resuscitation. He put his hand down on his father's forehead and started to stroke it.

"Get your hands off of me, you idiot," he said, throwing his son's hand back with flick of his hand. "Get on back to where you belong."

"Where's that, Dad? I belong here with you."

"Get on out of here now. Never could tell you a goddamn thing."

"What's going on, Dad? This isn't like you? What's wrong?"

"Nothing's wrong with me. It's you idiots that are all trying to tell me what to do. I'm my own boss and have been for years. Don't need any snot-nosed kids trying to wet-nurse me.

I got off the tit a long time ago. No wonder Bull Oliver didn't want anybody comin' around."

Just when it seemed that nothing would help calm the old man down, the doctor stopped in and told the nurse to get a sleeping pill. Jack didn't see him, but Jim was able to persuade his father to take the pill the nurse had finally brought. Slowly the old man relaxed and lay back on his pillow, thinking.

Fucking people in these places try to run your business and tell you what they think you want to hear. Sure a different world today, as Bake and Roc would say, but some things never change. People always trying to tell you how to live and what you could and couldn't do.

Mathews had been in the hospital back in the States near where Jack had been healing and recuperating. His doctor had said that the crippled hand would be as good as new in six months after surgery in the California hospital. But it was still stiff, and the fingers curled in the same place, frozen in place. It didn't look like it would ever be any different. Jack hadn't believed the doctor for a minute and thought he knew bullshit when he heard it in Hawaii.

Mathews, who had lost a foot and part of his leg in the foxhole where Bake had been hit along with Greene and Kelly, was already back in the States, too. His stomach wounds were healing well. It was his leg that was giving him the problem. Jack had gone to see Mathews in the amputee ward on Mare Island just outside of San Francisco as soon as he was able to leave the hospital and get there. He found him confined to his bed and the ward.

"Hey, Mathews," he said after they'd exchanged hellos and what-you-been-up-tos and had been introduced to the man in the next bed, "what can I do for you guys?"

"Bring us in a bottle of whiskey."

"You mean they won't let you have a bottle of whiskey in this joint?" Jack asked and laughed. It figured that a bottle of whiskey would be what Mathews wanted, though. He'd left that foot on Iwo Jima and had just come from talking with the surgeon about how things were coming with his leg and what they'd have to do with it.

"Sonuvabitch, told me it was healing real well," Mathews said, laughing that contagious laugh of his that spread from ear to ear and lighted up wherever he let it go. "Then he told me that it was a bit too long to get a good fit for a new foot. Said he needed seven inches. I told him I wouldn't mind that myself.

"He said he'd like to take more of my leg, and I said, 'If that's what you need to do, let's do it.' And I asked him when. He said, 'In the morning.' I said, 'Damn.' He said, 'Morning it is.'"

"They took the seven inches from mine when they took the foot," Jack said. "I'll get the whiskey for you."

He hid a bottle of Jack Daniels bourbon in his trousers later that evening and smuggled it past the guards who kept a close watch for contraband. Mathews and his buddy in the next bed got drunk that night and Mathews didn't have the other part of his leg cut off for another week. The doctor was pissed off about the whiskey, Mathews said, and the staff tried to find out where the whiskey came from and who brought it in.

"Fuckin' idiots," Mathews told Jack later. "They told us we couldn't have whiskey in the hospital and then wanted us to tell who brought us the whiskey. Can you imagine that? I told them I didn't know why we couldn't have it and said it must be the tooth fairy that brought it in. The bottle was under my pillow when I woke up one morning, I told them. That's all I knew. And I figured if it was there, we could drink it. Wouldn't you think?"

The old man laughed and thought maybe he'd find something under his pillow when he woke a bit later. He thought he could feel something there and tried to reach for it. Just as he was about to touch whatever was there, a Jap soldier put his rifle with a long, wicked-looking bayonet on it right up next to Jack's head and held it tight.

"You dlie, Mlarine," the Jap said with a maniacal laugh. "Flucking Flranklin Rlooslvelt eat shit and bark at the moon. New York Yankees eat shit, too."

"You're right about them damn Yankees," the old man said aloud. "They eat shit and bark at the moon just like that fuckin' old Tojo."

Two more Jap soldiers appeared and poked at him with their rifles and long bayonets. Jack'd wrapped his hand with a bandage Doc Childers had given him. And his shoulder and foot wounds had been dressed. Jack was thankful for the morphine. He had no pain and yet seemed alert and aware of everything that was going on. Maybe that was not so good. He was afraid of what was going to happen. The Jap soldiers motioned with their rifles and bayonets for him to stand up. That wasn't going to be easy. His leg had already begun to stiffen up, and his right arm was in a sling. He looked around and saw that he was a couple of hundred yards behind the rest of the squad, cut off from it by the three Japs that came out behind him and now had him as their prisoner. Jack didn't like that idea. He knew what the Japs did to their prisoners, although none of them ever lived to tell about it. He'd heard Marines screaming out in the night after they'd got cut off from their outfits and heard about men finding bodies with tongues cut out and blood all over their faces or cocks cut off and shoved in their mouths. And he was afraid that something of the kind would happen to him unless he could somehow escape.

He kept quiet, pulled himself up and took in the sweeping view he had of the small volcanic island. Mount Suribachi rose up off to the south and Old Glory still flew from the highest point. He motioned to the Jap soldiers and pointed off to the flag. He'd never forget as long as he lived that morning when he and thousands of other Marines had looked up and seen the flag proudly wave to them in the distance. The roar had gone up so loud that Japs burrowed away in the hundreds of caves on The Rock must have heard and peeked out of their holes to see what was going on. These three assholes must've heard the roar, too, he thought. One of them prodded him with the end of a bayonet to get moving.

From his current vantage point near Hill 362A where he'd been hit, Jack looked back toward the beach. He was amazed that he was still alive sixteen days after D-Day. He was two weeks into his nineteenth year but couldn't remember what it was like to be eighteen. That was so young, so naïve, so much different. Ships still dotted the horizon, and the beach was littered with tanks and trucks and other material that had been hit with mortars or artillery from the entrenched Japanese. With the fields of fire and the well-fortified positions, it seemed impossible that the Marines had been able to move this far. And that was only across the island at the narrowest point of just more than a mile, south to Suribachi and then north less than halfway to the other end of the five-and-a-half-mile-long island. There was still a ways to go before they reached the sea to the north. But they'd get there. Nobody doubted that. It was just when and at what price.

On his feet now, Jack limped along with the three Jap soldiers. He could see that escape was going to be very difficult. He obviously couldn't run. Nor could he take on three Japs with his wounds. They stopped at a small opening in the side of a small hill and motioned for Jack to go on into the hole. He looked at the hole and fell backward, pretending to pass out. They might shoot him or stick a bayonet through him, he realized, but he thought he might be able to grab one around the neck when he got close and get his pistol to shoot the other two. No way in hell did he intend to go down to the bowels of the island. His body was tense, ready to move into action, as he laid waiting for the Jap to get close enough. Jack could smell the Japs and waited, feeling his heart thump in his chest like a trip hammer. The smell of fish heads and rice and garlic mixed with shit, piss and sweat hit his nose, and he reached for the first Jap soldier's throat and started choking him.

"It's okay, Dad," Jim said, taking his father's hands as he sat up in the bed and reached out with both hands. "It's okay."

"No, it isn't okay. You don't know nothing. I was goin' to get those bastards until you stopped me. And now I've got to shit."

"I think you might already have done that, Dad," Jim said softly. He'd smelled the bowel movement for quite a while as he sat dozing in the chair but wasn't going to disturb his father and get him changed. "Let me get the nurses to change your bed and clean you up."

"Nothin' to clean up. But I've got to get up now, I tell you. And I don't mean maybe. I've got to get up right now. Is that clear?"

The old man had swung his feet over the side of the bed rail and was struggling to sit up. Jim hit the call button and lifted his father's feet up and back over the bed rail. Melanie walked in and went to the other side of the bed.

"I think we'd better get the bed changed and get you cleaned up," she said. "It's not good for you to lay in that."

"I'm not laying in anything. You're crazy. Get away from me. Tend to your own business, and I'll tend to mine. What're they trying to do to me?"

While Melanie was going for help and what they'd need to get everything cleaned up, Jim tried to calm his father and talked softly about him resting and getting to feel better. It had little effect. The old man didn't want anyone near him and would try to brush Jim away with a feeble backhanded swat. One of the nurses took him by the arm and guided him toward the curtain and another woman who had come into the room.

"This is Sheila. She's the head nurse. She'll get you a cup of coffee or something to drink while we change your father's bed."

Jim turned back to the bed and said, "They're going to change the bed, Dad. I'll see you in a few minutes."

"They're not going to do anything. I'm going to get out of this bed and shit and get rid of all this stuff. You're all a bunch of goddamn idiots for what you're tryin' to do to me."

"We're all trying to help you."

"Help me, my ass. You're trying to kill me, that's what you're trying to do. Trying to get rid of me. You hurt me anymore and I'm going to call the skipper. Somebody dropped me on the goddamn floor. I'm hurt, and I'll get you all arrested. Now get out of here, all of you."

Before Jim had turned to leave, the old man reached for his nose, pulled the oxygen line from his nostrils and tossed it aside. Then he reached for the tube running up through his nose. Jim reached one side of the bed and the duty nurse the other side before the old man had jerked on the tube. Both of them took one of his hands in both of theirs and held on. He'd wiggle out of their grasp and reach back for the tube in his nose or his IV or an arterial line they had put in an artery just above his wrist. All the while, his eyes flashed hotly and he swore profusely.

"Get your goddamn hands off of me, you idiots!" the old man hollered.

"That's enough, Dad," Jim said. "Quit acting like a jerk."

"I'll act anyway I want to. You idiots are the ones that are acting like jerks."

The other nurse slipped in front of Jim and said, "Have some coffee and we'll take care of your father."

He had no more than got to the brightly lit inner circle where all the staff had desks and phones and could watch over patients in the rooms that encircled the intensive care unit's outer walls than he heard his father lash out at the two nurses.

"You're hurting me, goddamnit."

"No, Mr. Britton, we're not hurting you; you're hurting you. We're trying to take care of you and get your bed changed."

"You're not trying to do anything. Just get away from me — oh, oh, you're hurting me. Now quit that, you're hurting me, goddamnit. What is wrong with you people?"

Jim looked at the head nurse and back at the room. A male nurse hurried to the room.

"He'll be okay. They'll take care of him. Let's get you some coffee."

They stopped in a small room nestled between two patient rooms part way around the outer circle. But they could still hear the old man cry out or cuss somebody.

"Quit that, goddamnit. I mean it. You're hurting me, you fuckin' idiots."

Jim winced every time he heard his father swear or cry out in pain. Once when the pain in his father's voice sounded almost unbearable, Jim jumped and cringed. The head nurse tried to keep him talking and explained, as had the other nurse, that what his father was going through was not uncommon in the elderly. The behavior happened all the time and wasn't something to be too concerned about in the big picture. It'd pass with the night. The compound clock showed a little after three a.m. Nearly three hours until the sun would come up.

"I'll make it," Jim said, "with the help of God and a few of Dad's Marines."

Some fifteen minutes later, the nurses were finished. The tube in his nose, the IV for the nitroglycerin, even the nose line for the oxygen that'd been hanging down from his neck, were all gone. The arterial line was still intact, but Jim looked around in amazement.

"What happened?" he asked. "His face is clean."

"You father was going to pull the tube from his nose and the A-line that's taped into an artery. He's quite strong and might have gotten the job done. But we called Dr. Yasunaga and told him what was going on. He said we might as well remove the tube to his stomach but leave the arterial line until morning. That gives us the most accurate blood pressure reading, and we need that for the rest of the night. So the A-line and the catheter are still there."

"Why are his hands tied?"

"He was going to pull the catheter and the A-line out. So we put the mittens on and tie them together to keep him from doing that. But you'll have to watch him. He's trying to get the mittens off. I've got a couple of pills to help him sleep, if we can get him to take them."

"I'm not taking those pills, I've told you before," the old man said through clinched teeth. "They're not the same kind of pills I take at home. That's what this idiot says. I don't know what she's trying to pull, but I'm not falling for it. And I'm going to call the skipper about the way you've all been treating me. You're all mean. You hurt me."

Both Melaine and Jim tried talking calmly and explaining that nobody was trying to hurt him, that they were trying to help him.

"Ha," he said. "I'd sure as hell hate to see you when you were planning to hurt me. Betcha couldn't do a damn bit better."

"We had to change your bed and clean you up."

"That's a lie. You didn't change a thing."

"Why are you sitting there naked, then, Dad?"

"I'm not naked. I wasn't going to wear one of their stupid nightshirts. They look stupid. Told them to get one of the ones out of the dresser over there. Too dumb to get it. Finally somebody went over and got this one. Wasn't going to wear one of those stupid nightshirts."

"You don't have a nightshirt on, Dad."

"You're dumb as a box of rocks and blind as a bat. Why don't you go home and take this woman out of here, away from me? I don't want nothin' from her."

The old man absolutely refused to take anything from either Melanie or the aide who'd been helping her; the big old whore was the one that smacked him up side the head when they were wrestling him around and hurting him, he knew. He'd seen her before. She'd just taken on five of his buddies at the whorehouse down in Honolulu where Chernowski led them when they had liberty in Honolulu from Camp Tarawa one time.

She was a big woman, maybe five feet, eight inches tall and well over two hundred pounds. They all stayed in line and watched as she took care of each one of the young Marines for five bucks a crack and in record time. When one would finish, the big whore would reach her hand in her cunt, throw the semen in a bucket by the bed and yell, "Next!"

Jack didn't know how the others felt, but he didn't like what he was seeing. Watching his buddies screw the big whore right in front of him and them seeing her scoop out the semen and throw it in a bucket reminded him of a story he'd heard in high school about a bunch of kids catching Georgia Ann Wilson, a mildly retarded woman who lived out on a farm with her parents, and gang-banging her in a parked car out on a country road late one Saturday night. After taking care of the first three or four, Georgia Ann sat up, so the story went, and said, "No more until I get a Pepsi." And somebody raced off into town to get her a Pepsi from the all-night garage and diner. Jack had always thought that was just a story guys told to try to impress other kids. He hadn't thought much of what he'd heard and never believed it really happened. But he couldn't get Georgia Ann Wilson and the story out of his mind. It had a life of its own. When it came Jack's turn at the old whore, he turned and walked away. He couldn't get a hard-on and didn't want to take his turn, anyway. She could keep the five bucks.

"But I want these stupid gloves off," the old man said, putting both hands between his legs and trying to untie the strings that kept the mittens on. "Get them off right now or give me my five bucks back."

"Tell you what, Dad, you take these pills and we'll take the gloves off."

"Take 'em off."

"Will you take the pills?"

"They're not the same thing I've been taking. They're pulling something on me. I don't know what it is, but I'm not falling for their tricks."

"No tricks, Dad. They're just the generic for what you've been taking at home. Trust me."

"Take these gloves off," he said, moving his mittened hands together in his lap.

"Will you take the pills?"

"Get these damn things off my hands. What's the matter with you people?"

"We don't want you to hurt yourself, Dad. They took the tube out of your nose and they took the IV out, and you don't have to take the oxygen and have that tickling your nose unless you need it or want it. You'll probably feel better without the IV. Your heart must be okay. But you've still got the arterial line in your arm to monitor your blood pressure. Your doctor said they could take that out in the morning. Right now they still need to monitor your blood pressure, and the arterial line is the most accurate way to do it."

"That's bullshit. Get rid of that fuckin' doctor, too. He's been feeding me bullshit all the way along. Ever since I met him. Fuckin' Jap. Gettin' rid of all of you. If you don't all get away from me, I'm going to call the skipper. You can't treat people like you're treating me."

"We're trying to help you, Dad," Jim said, holding the string of one of the mitts to keep his father from wiggling his hand out of the mitt while holding onto it with the other one. "You're not cooperating very much. You've still got the catheter, and you don't want to pull it out. I'll guarantee you that wouldn't be pleasant."

"You just want to boss me around. That's all it is. You want to tell me what to do. Let me tell you something, sonny boy, I'm my own goddamn boss and have been for a helluva long time. I'll get out of here and go where I want to, when I want to. Do you understand that, boy?"

Jim laughed and said, "That sounds a little like me when I was a kid in high school and thought I should get to be my own boss and do whatever I wanted to. You and I have had several conversations about that. Sometimes you have to go by the rules."

"Not when they're stupid rules like they have here at Great Lakes," the old man said.

When he was at Great Lakes Naval Hospital north of Chicago, wounded veterans and other patients were only allowed to travel fifty miles on liberty. But it was ninety miles home on the bus. Jack and many of the others went home every time they got liberty, regardless of the fifty-mile limit. Semper Fi, Mac. Hooray for me and fuck you. He'd never been asked for his pass that specified how far he could travel. And when he didn't get back from liberty, which was granted every other day, someone who had liberty but didn't take it would sleep in his bed. They all did that for each other and never had a problem. The only problem was getting back in the gate. Sailors pulling duty on the gate would report Marines who came back late or over leave, but the Marines would let all Marines in no matter what. Sometimes Jack had had to wait four hours for the change of the guard for the Marines to relieve the sailors on the gate. It was a bother, but it was something they all had to do when somebody's stupid rules got in the way.

"Stupid rules," the old man said.

He'd been in a Quonset-hut hospital in Hawaii where the wounded were fenced in, waiting for a transfer to the hospital in Aiea for the operation on his arm. Some of the wounded had found a hole in the fence or someone had made one that could be covered back up, and they often went AWOL for various purposes and then came back in the same way. They had to be back in the evening, though. One time Jack went out and into a naval station to see an old family friend from back home who was a submariner and took him down in a docked submarine. The old man shuddered and drew his hands together, wiggling them into a fist and out of the mittens that tied his hands together. He didn't like to be tied up.

And he hated to be cooped up. The submarine was unbelievably narrow. A person could get claustrophobia in there, down under the sea in those cramped quarters. Later, it began to rain and really rained with almost gale-like force. Jack stayed with his friend until he knew he had to get back before it was found out that he was AWOL. It was only then that Jack discovered that no one could get out of the gate unless he had a special pass. He waited until the downpour was at its highest and the guards were getting really drenched and miserable. It reminded him of the cold, rainy nights on Iwo Jima when the mortar fire sporadically throughout the night made it even more miserable and gut-wrenching than this night. And the only guards out there were Japs or other Marines who would blow you away if you were roaming around in the rain.

So he hobbled to the gate through the driving rain, shouted to the guards that he had a pass but had to make an appointment and kept on hobbling right past them. They yelled something he couldn't hear or didn't intend to hear, and he kept on moving. He was in uniform and knew they wouldn't shoot him, so he didn't stop. He made it back to the hospital and through the hole in the fence without incident but felt sorry for the guards. They didn't know what to do and were undoubtedly wet and miserable. Since he never heard anything about him not stopping at the gate at four in the morning, he figured that the two of them just said, "Let's forget about it and not report it and get into trouble for letting someone out without a pass." That's what Jack and most of the wounded men around him would have done. After the war, the veterans didn't give a damn about regulations anymore. They'd done what they'd been asked to do, been killed and maimed beyond their wildest expectations but had won the war and wanted to get on with life without the rules and regulations of stateside military duty.

"*Don't fence me in,*'" the old man began singing an old Forties' tune in an off-key voice as he remembered it, "'*Don't fence me in because I've got what'll make you jump the fence, what'll make you jump the fence. ...*'"

Jim had heard his father sing the song in the same off-key voice when he'd had a few drinks and turned melancholy and had always wondered what it was that would make you jump the fence. His father just laughed, shook his head when he'd asked him what it was that'd make anybody jump the fence and said, "Whatever you want it to be, I reckon."

"Now I want to tell you idiots something," the old man said, looking up at his son and only giving the nurse a quick glance through half-glazed eyes. There was a troubled look, a somewhat scared look in his eyes. At times the look went blank, into a sort of nothingness. Then he'd come back, eyes flashing anger. "I'm going to smack you up side the head, if you don't get out of here and leave me alone. I want these fuckin' gloves off, and I want them off now. And get her out of here before she tries to hurt me again. She's mean. Dumber 'n hell, too."

"Take those pills," Jim said, "and I'll take them off."

The old man stared angrily at his son and said, "You're real dumb. What is it that you don't understand about gettin' these goddamn gloves off of me?"

"I understand that you're going to keep the goddamn gloves on until you start behaving and quit trying to pull those lines out and hurt yourself," Jim said, speaking back to his father now in the same tone of voice. "You understand, goddamnit?"

"Don't talk to me that way."

"Don't talk to me that way."

"I want these gloves off of me, and I want them off now."

The old man raised his arms and turned away, doubling his left fist and pulling at the glove with his right hand until his hand was almost out. He was already moving his hand to the arterial line in his right arm when Jim grabbed the glove and guided his father's left hand back into the glove. He twisted and turned, shouting, "Get your goddamn hands off of me. I'll —"

Jim held the glove with his right hand and slapped his father sharply with his left hand. The old man's head snapped back and a hurt look came into his eyes. He stared at his son.

"Get a hold of yourself, Dad," Jim said. "You're not helping anything."

"You're mean. I never hit my father in my life."

"I'm sorry I slapped you, Dad. But I thought maybe it'd bring you around."

The mortar fire was heavy. Jack had just jumped in the shell hole with Bake and Roc. Eastin, the Guadalcanal and Bougainville veteran with a Silver Star from the first and a Purple Heart and a Bronze Star from the second and uncanny luck and grit to do whatever necessary to gain the objective, slid in the hole. He didn't have to make the Iwo Jima landing but had volunteered because he liked combat and thought he could help with his experience. Between mortar barrages, two Marines were bringing back from the front a Marine with his whole face shot off. It was just a mass of blood. The man was unrecognizable

"It's Scotty," Bake said. "That's Wilson and Robinson carrying him."

"Scotty?" Jack said, his voice raising and cracking as he mouthed the name and rose to his knees. His M-1 rifle hung limply in his right hand. "Fuckin' Scotty?"

Scotty was one of two men in the platoon who wanted to be pro baseball players. He was a short, stocky kid from Georgia who played third base and could hit the ball a mile. Scotty was still breathing, but he was a mass of blood. Jack trembled slightly and stared in disbelief. He couldn't recognize the guy he'd played baseball with for months back at Camp Tarawa in Hawaii. They'd talked about their favorite teams, the Cubs and the Cardinals, playing baseball as kids and how Scotty thought he had a chance to make the big leagues. He was a third baseman who guarded the line like it was Fort Knox and made diving stops of smashes just over the bag or to his left, knocked down hard line drives like the Cardinals' Pepper Martin and saved ball game after ball game with his glove and his arm. Nothing fancy, but not much got by him. And he could hit a ton.

"Snap out of it," Eastin said as he smacked Jack across

the face with a quick backhand. "You're going into shock. I've seen that happen before, and you can't do it. Snap out of it now."

And it worked. Jack shook his head and was okay after that. But he still couldn't believe that mess was Scotty. He died later, as did another baseball buddy, Lefty. He was a speedy little outfielder from California whose heart made up for what he lacked in size either playing baseball or fighting the Japs. Both gone, along with their dreams of big-league careers.

"Get these things off my hands," the old man said, raising his head up to look at his son. The eyes looked old and tired, washed out and dim. They'd flash anger or hurt now and then, but mostly the looks were of confusion or doubt more and more. "What the hell?"

Jack leaned down and kissed Betty again as she lay there waiting to be taken away to the funeral home and prepared for burial. He couldn't understand how this had happened so suddenly. It had been one thing back in the war to see people there one minute and gone the next. This was normal life. Betty had felt good most of the time while she was pregnant. They enjoyed being together and planning for the baby. One night a week or so before the baby was due, they had a candlelight dinner to celebrate the coming of the new addition. He pan fried a ribeye steak, baked a potato and made a garden salad for them. He drank red wine with dinner; she drank grape juice. After they finished eating, they sat at the table and talked until the candle burned out.

"I can hardly wait to hold this baby," Betty said, holding out her hand to take Jack's. "It wasn't long ago that I was so worried about losing you. And now not only have I got you, but we're going to have a beautiful baby, the first of many."

"Whoa, not so fast. The first of many? I'd like to have more kids, too. But let's wait until I graduate and find a job. That's at least two more years."

"I didn't mean right away. We've got the rest of our lives. But you'd better get in there and start studying or there won't be two more years. You've got a couple of papers to finish before the baby is born, don't you?"

The sky was just beginning to lighten the eastern sky when the old man began to settle down a bit and drifted off to a light sleep. He could see the vague outline of Hill 362A and a Jap bunker directly to his front, but he was almost certain that they'd knocked it out when the replacement lieutenant who'd only been with the platoon for three days had led the charge up the hill and had his legs blown off by a mortar round. Jack had later heard that the lieutenant had pulled himself to a standing position on his stumps, using an M-1 rifle to balance himself, and rallied what was left of his platoon to storm the Jap position. If that happened, Jack didn't see it, didn't think it was possible. He only remembered seeing the lieutenant prop himself up on his elbow and wave the platoon on with the other hand. "Go get 'em, men. Go get 'em."

And Dubois led the way as the Marines jumped up and ran forward, crying and screaming, "Let's get them sonsabitches." In ten minutes the pillboxes were silenced for good. Three Japs came running from one of them after a Marine with a flamethrower had shot a burst through the slip-like opening in the pillbox putting out the most fire and rounds from five

different M-1s and a BAR cut them down before they'd taken
five steps away from a pillbox. Later, everyone took cover and
checked on the lieutenant. The corpsman had tied tourniquets
around his legs and shot him up with morphine. But he was
aware of what the Marines had done in the ten minutes after
he'd been hit. He'd heard the crying and screaming as they
stormed the hill to take care of the pillbox.

"You men did a helluva job," he said, lying on the ground
on a stretcher with four men ready to move him out for the
beach. "It's been an honor for me to have led you in combat.
Looks like I've lost that opportunity and you've lost a damn
good lieutenant. Give 'em hell, boys. This is some expensive real
estate, but we've got to have it."

Melanie came to the door and motioned for Jim to come
out. She had a slip of paper in her hand and said, "I don't know
what I'd have done without you last night and wanted to give
you a breakfast certificate down in the cafeteria. You can get
some rest for a while now, I think, and then go get a good breakfast. You deserve it."

"Thanks. It was quite an interesting night," Jim said. "I don't
know about resting much, though. Too much coffee and too
much going on. I'm finishing reading a novel to get my mind settled
down now. But breakfast sounds good. I'm hungry. I don't know
what I'd have done without you, either. Thanks for all your help."

The nurse stepped up and gave him a hug and went off
duty. Jim walked back into the room. His father was uncov-
ered, lying on his side, legs drawn up to his chest in a fetal position. He looked up at Jim standing quietly at the side of the
wagon. He could see the butterflies flittering about over the

garden and could smell the flowers. Aunt Maggie and some others were there but were fading and seemed to be walking right into the fence and out of sight. He raised his head slightly to see if he could see where they had gone

"How you doing, Dad?" Jim asked.

"Doin' good. I'm lookin' for your mother and Bake and Roc. They're around here somewhere. I just feel it. Goin' to be good to see them again."

"Think you're goin' to see them soon?"

"Won't be long. We ain't got much more time to talk about the Marine Corps, though. I'm not worth a damn. Can't do anything. Had a terrible night last night. Couldn't sleep a bit."

Jim smiled.

"That's for sure," he said. "I couldn't either."

"Did I keep you awake?"

"Oh, no. I just couldn't sleep with everything going on."

"I'm awfully tired, Jimbo. I'm going to sleep awhile now, I think. But hand me that rose, will you? I just want to smell it, see if I can."

Jim handed him a flower from the vase on the chest by the bed. His father held it to his nose and smiled. "*Reach me a gentian, give me a torch!*" the old man began as he held the rose. "*Let me guide myself with the blue, forked touch of a flower down the darker and darker stairs, where blue is darkened on blueness even where Persephone goes, from the frosted September to the sightless realm where darkness is awake upon the dark.*' How's that?"

"That's fine, Dad. I've never heard you recite that. Who is it?"

"D.H. Lawrence," the old man said and laughed. "Don't you think that's appropriate? That I'd be reduced to old D.H.'s '*Bavarian Gentians*' at the end. Not William Cullen Bryant's '*Thanatopsis.*' Not Dylan Thomas' '*Do Not Go Gentle Into That Good*

Night.' Not William Carlos Williams' '*Tract.*' Not the Bible's '*Twenty-fifth Psalm.*' Not even the '*Marine Corps Hymm.*' But Lawrence's obscure reference to some goddamn old blue flowers? My Aunt Maggie used to grow them in her flower garden when I was a kid. I loved them."

Two streaks of tears ran quietly down Jim's cheeks that he could feel but couldn't be seen in the early-morning light filtering into the room. "Get a little rest, Dad" he said. "I'll get some breakfast downstairs and be back up shortly."

The old man smiled and had drifted off to sleep when Jim came back from breakfast and read for just a few minutes before falling off to sleep himself. When he woke an hour later, Jack Britton had taken a turn for the worse. His body was swollen from the tips of his fingers down to the ends of his toes. His breathing became more labored, and he coughed, his chest heaved and crackled. The day nurses were working on him and calling the doctor when Jim awakened.

"Don't bother the corpsman," the old man said, whispering hoarsely. "I'm not going to make her now, boys. Fuckin' incoming all over the place. You can't dig me out this time."

The line on the heart monitor went flat, and the old man looked at peace.